THE SPIDER

CRYPTID CHRONICLES

SCOTT FREER

This is a work of fiction. Names, characters, places, and incidents are products of the author's imagination or are used fictitiously and are not to be construed as real. Any resemblance to actual events, locations, organizations, or persons, living or dead, is entirely coincidental.

World Castle Publishing, LLC
Pensacola, Florida
Copyright © Scott Freer 2019
Paperback ISBN: 9781951642068
eBook ISBN: 9781951642075
First Edition World Castle Publishing, LLC, November 25, 2019
http://www.worldcastlepublishing.com
Licensing Notes
Cover: Karen Fuller
Editor: Maxine Bringenberg

"The oldest and strongest emotion of mankind is fear, and the oldest and strongest kind of fear is fear of the unknown." ~H.P. Lovecraft.

THE BEGINNING

The roaring cracks of thunder echoed through the sky, flashing aqua lights through the broken down windows and cracked walls like a sporadic police siren. The torrent of rain crashed down upon the roof like a thousand arrows. The broken and beaten arcade had seen its share of decay and dread, but even in a history filled with so much blood as that of Mark's Game-And-Stop, this night would leave a red stained memory.

The once shiny white walls had become a moldy, decayed green. On the floor were puddles of green slime, yet no one could know from where they came. Large rodents and spiders roamed these halls as freely as the people outside, seemingly ignorant of the horrid memories this detestable place held for so many.

Erik clutched tightly against the silver half-heart pendant hanging from his necklace. His eyes began to focus once more, another crack of lightning shaking the earth beneath his feet. He clasped a thick, sweaty hand to his leg. He could feel the blood flowing freely out of the stumped bottom, but he couldn't stop his stride, even for a moment.

He limped his way as quickly as his broken and beaten bones would take him towards the beautiful sight of the EXIT sign at the end of the inky-black, mossy green hallway. As his hand dragged along the wall he was using to hold himself from falling, he could practically feel the years of decay that had overrun the once great arcade of the town of Witchern, Ontario. Some sick part of him wondered what the fuzzy, almost lifelike substance beneath his fingers had been, but he couldn't bring himself to stop and look.

Suddenly something ripped from the wall, sending Erik falling to the floor. He tried catching himself on his arms, but the bruises and gashes all over his body had weakened him so much that he couldn't hold the weight. He felt his chin smash against a cracked tile on the once checkerboard patterned floor, which now resembled more of a green and dark green pattern.

He let loose his grip on the old "Happy Birthday Ricky!" banner that had been the reason for his fall. The rips and tears along the banner only made him think more on the wonderful parties that they must've had here all those years ago. He stood himself up, using the wall for balance, and pressed on.

His mind pushed him forward, beaded

sweat causing a stinging sensation through his eyes. Each step seemed to take ages of agony before his foot planted itself to the floor. He wondered, frightened if escape was any closer than—

A scream burst out, breaking him from thought. It came from somewhere behind him, somewhere far away, he hoped. He instinctively turned towards the sound, but it wasn't the only sound that met his ears. He began to hear jittering scratches quickly approaching, thousands of them, their long legs scratching whatever surface the little devils decided they'd attach themselves to. He gripped the bloody leg tightly and forced himself to run. Each step he took felt like a hot iron pressing itself tightly against his ankle—or rather, where his ankle *should* be. He pressed on.

He felt the sudden irresistible urge to glance over his shoulder. He tried his best to avoid the urge, to press on towards the beautiful safety of the EXIT sign no more

CRYPTID CHRONICLES: THE SPIDER

than ten meters away. The urge overtook him and he looked, and wished he hadn't.

Thousands—no millions—of red eyes were crawling quickly towards him, the tiny legs on their bodies scratching the floor, and their wide open chelicera fangs snapping shut over and over again. He felt his heart beating faster than he thought possible. He turned back and sprinted as best he could, trying furiously to ignore the pain, the throbbing hell that had become his leg.

He couldn't have been more than a few feet away from the door when a new sound chilled him; a hushed whisper. Like a calm wind, it resonated throughout the arcade until it hit Erik's ears. The sound sent a chill running through every nerve in his body. The shock made him lose his footing, landing face first in a rather large pile of the slimy green substance that was scattered over the floors. He only hoped it wasn't fresh.

He pulled around, prepared to protect himself from the thousands of fist-sized arachnids in whatever way he could when suddenly…nothing. They were gone. Not a single one of those red eyes was staring at him in the cold dark hallway. He held his breath, holding the hope that he might make it out of there in one piece. He waited, for what, he didn't know, but he felt that if he ran now, something would get him. So he watched the shadows, but nothing came. The silence screamed a thousand deafening notes in his bloody ears. He could feel his legs moving on their own, wanting to run away, and he finally allowed it, turning towards the door, reaching out towards the handle. But what his hand met was not the handle to the exit door. Nor was it anywhere near the door itself.

Suddenly, a drop of green slime fell to his hand. The stinging pain from the fresh venom ran through his arm and up. He slowly felt his body numbing, with a pain like a thousand bolts of lightning were piercing him. He felt the sensation run through his body until he couldn't hold himself anymore. Erik fell to the ground, motionless, though his eyes could still see the horror before him.

The terrifyingly large creature slowly descended from the tall ceiling towards him. As those horrifyingly enormous red eyes lowered ever closer to him, her enormous, spiny white legs shaking gleefully, he watched with his fading, foggy vision as the world slowly darkened to an inky, black shadow.

The Reunion

"Welcome to Witchern!" The sign roared past them as they drove down the two lane highway into the small country town. Sarah watched as the bright green fields flew past at eighty miles per hour. She fiddled with the small golden pendant hanging from her golden chain. It reminded her of the last time she'd seen her brother, just before she left for school.

***

"Study hard and no boys!" Her brother had said to her. He tried to keep the stern look to replace the one that should have been from their absent father, but his boyish smile snuck its way through every time.

"No parties, back to the dorm by ten every night, and don't do anything you wouldn't do." She finished his checklist for him, trying not to sound too pleased about leaving. "I'm only going for two years...it's not like I'm moving away forever."

"Well, two years without my personal 'little devil' will be difficult!" Her brother would always call her the little devil to break the tension, but it almost never worked. "Who's gonna get me into all kinds of shenanigans while you're gone?"

"Please, you and Joey get into more 'shenanigans' than anyone in town. With you two asshats around, I think my share will be taken care of." She gave him a wink.

The blue cab slowly turned the corner. It honked, and the tanned driver waved the two down from the window.

"That has to be him." Her older brother waved back, and the cab waited for them at the edge of the sidewalk. "So you've got everything? Got your passport, your boarding pass, all your clothes, your carry-on?"

"Yes!" She shoved him lightly with a laugh. "I've got everything. Just help me take it to the cab already!"

"All right, all right! Stop pushing!"

The two of them meticulously put everything in the trunk of the cab. They would always treat it like a Tetris game together, trying to make it as perfectly aligned as possible. The two laughed at the end, looking at their work of art.

"That's a full line! We win!" Her brother yelled into the wind.

"No one can beat us!" She mimicked her brother's shout.

"Well, all aboard, I suppose." Her brother scratched at the back of his head uncomfortably.

"Come on, what is it?" She said, crossing her arms at him.

14

"What is what?"

"You always scratch your head like that when you're hiding something. I *know* you."

"All right. Well, I kinda got you a going away present." He pulled out a small, white, ornate box from his pocket.

"I thought we weren't doing this!" She scolded him, but found herself excitedly reaching for the box with both hands and opening it. Inside was a small golden pendant in the shape of a small half-heart. Along the edge were small cracks, as if it the other side was chipped off. Alongside it was a long golden chain. She pulled it out gently and threaded it through the looped metal latch on the heart.

"It's beautiful," she said, in awe of the way the bright sunlight reflected off the face of the heart. "Wait, how much did this cost?"

"Don't you worry about the price. And don't even try to keep asking, because I'm not telling."

She scowled at him, but inside her heart

was a burning flurry. She reached back and tied the latch, dropping the pendant down on her chest. It hung a little low, but she imagined she could get it adjusted first thing when they landed.

"Look, I've got one too." He pulled out a silver half-heart necklace from under his shirt. "Now we're always together. You've got half of a heart, and I've got the other half!"

"I think that only works if they're the same heart, genius." She looked at him over the frames of her glasses.

"Look, I'm workin' with what I got. Give me a break here. Besides, gold is your favorite color, so we're all happy here!"

"I guess you're right — we each have half of the other's heart."

"Together forever!" Her brother let loose a wide, toothy smile. Sarah always felt like his smile brightened up the day even more than the sun itself could.

"Together for — "

HONK

The driver pressed down on the horn and waved at them again, beckoning for them to hurry.

"Now go on, you'll miss the plane. Go!"

Her brother smiled his smile again. She opened the cab door and waved at him. A strange goodbye. They each had half of the other's heart on their chest. She hoped that two years from now they could leave the little town together for good.

***

They hit a bump on the road and Sarah's vision snapped back to the present. They were passing the big farms on the outside of town. Sarah waved at each animal as they passed. It had become a tradition for her to say "Hi" to every animal she saw, no matter how scary or how small.

"...and that ends our story for the day." The cab driver turned the dial away from the news show and put on some classical music for the road.

"Damn shame," he muttered beneath his voice.

"What is?" Sarah asked, sliding the necklace beneath her bright red sweater.

"Another pair o' missing youngins," the driver responded, glancing at her through his rear view mirror. "Damn shame."

"Yeah, damn shame." Sarah mirrored his expression. "Did you catch the names?"

"Nah, only 'eard it for a second. Two missin' as o' last week, 'aven't been found since."

"Wow, a week, eh? I hope they're okay—"

"Me too, lil' lady." The driver turned the corner. "Me too. Well, 'ere we are."

Sarah payed the man his money, plus a fair bit extra for the quiet ride she'd requested, and the cabby drove off down the road. She watched the red taillights for a moment until the cab turned the corner. She looked over the building before her; a small, red bricked building with windows all along the front. Looking briefly into them, she saw the patrons sitting neatly at their booths eating their breakfasts, or whatever they were having on that particular Thursday morning.

Something caught her eye flashing above her. The old, red neon sign brought back nostalgic memories of mischievous childhood acts beneath the tables and within the kitchen. She could see the name clear as day—Sal's Diner: The Canadian Way—yet the sign was showing its clear age, as several of the letters refused to illuminate any longer. She smiled to herself as she read out the "new" flashing sign atop the building.

"Sl Die: Te Candi Wa," she whispered to herself, hardy realizing that she had spoken aloud. She wondered what incantation she might have uttered when stringing those words together, then giggled at her imagination.

The small bell chimed as she pushed open the door. A small, very light ringing sounded through the rather small diner. Each person sitting at their booth or table — even the two boys simply standing at the counter, futilely attempting to flirt with the beautiful, young waitress — turned themselves excitedly towards the doorway, expecting the young, pretty girl who had left a long two years ago, returning from the hellish world of the "big city" as they knew it. Many smiles were lit across the customers' faces, though, in the crowd of smiling people happy to have their little Sarah back, were eyes of pure confusion. The small, thin girl, known for her long blonde hair, frilly yellow skirts, and pretty pink shoes, had been replaced by this new girl who seemed to prefer a dark grey or black to a bright yellow. Her shortened — yet still roughly shoulder length — hair was now a jet black, with hints of crimson sprinkled in like black fire. Her frilly yellow skirt was now a pair of dark blue jeans, which had been ripped and torn all along the legs, and her little pink shoes would have run in terror of the heavy pounding caused by her new black steel-toed combat boots.

There was a look of fear in the eyes of those who expected that same little eighteen-year-old girl to skip through the door like she had those years ago. This new, terrifying woman…she couldn't be Sarah.

"Hi everyone!" She said, her high-pitched voice bringing an even bigger shock to everyone. "I guess you missed me!" Her pretty, childlike smile brightened her face through the bangs of dark black hair that dripped into her eyes. She fiddled with the half-heart pendant around her neck anxiously.

"Sarah!" The pretty blonde waitress screamed, shoving the two boys to the side. Had he been a bit closer to her, Sarah might have heard one of them bragging about where the "pretty blonde" had touched him.

The girl pushed and shoved her way through the crowd of people making their way to greet the fresh new Sarah that had walked into the diner. Sarah could easily tell who had missed her most, but she wasn't surprised that her oldest and best friend would barrel her way in for the first hug.

"Bunny!" She screamed, jumping in for a hug. The two girls crashed together, knocking them both flat to the ground. Sarah struggled for air, praying to any god who was listening that none of her bones were broken. She could hear Lexi's laughter, even with her face buried in her shoulder. "Welcome back, Bunny!" She said, pulling them both to their feet. "Well, maybe you're not a bunny anymore." She gestured to her clothes.

"Hey, no one else is Bunny!" Sarah replied, punching her friend lightly in the shoulder. "I'm *always* Bunny, you're *always* Kitten."

"Yes, ma'am!" Lexi tried her best at a salute, but realized just how silly she looked in her work uniform.

Lexi abruptly realized how much time she was taking up and made her way back to the counter. The rest of the crowd slowly closed in on Sarah, greeting her with words of "Welcome back" and "City life musta changed you!" In a clearly joking manner. She got through the whole group without too much panic—which made her intensely proud of herself—and quietly approached the small booth that Lexi had prepared for the two of them.

She picked up the small sign that read "Booth saved for the animal crew! Find somewhere else!" Sarah snickered to herself, turning back to Lexi with the sign in hand. She gave her a thumbs up, and Lexi returned the gesture.

"Never were that polite, were you, Kitten?" She whispered to her.

"Oh, shut up and sit down!" Lexi whispered back.

She snickered again and took her seat, tossing the sign in her bag. She looked curiously out the window at the town she'd left those years ago. Strange dark clouds that nearly always hung over the town were still there, yet almost every day they seemed to refuse to bring down that much needed rainfall. She'd noticed thick air that stuck to her like butter on a hot day. She felt much heavier every time she took a breath, and a thousand times lighter when she released it. The cracking roads, destroyed buildings, and the empty streets made her remember the *real* reason she'd left this ghost of a town.

She searched through the empty streets, looking for that old blue pick-up truck she'd told her brother to scrap before she came home. She was already sure that he wouldn't do it, and expected to have had their little "argument" about it on their way here. But he hadn't been there holding that little rainbow sign that said her name, in pink letters. Nor did he surprise her with a jump from behind or a tickle attack to make her shriek while she dialed the number for the taxi company to request a ride home

Where is he…? she wondered.

"Whatcha lookin' at?" Lexi asked, dropping down on the seat opposite her like a sack of mud. "Town still looks the same, eh?"

"Exactly how I remember it," Sarah responded, a slight hint of disappointment in her voice.

"Is that bad?" Lexi asked, leaning against the window, bringing her feet up to the table.

"No, just a bit strange after being in 'the big city.' Somehow I expected it to be a bit more…lively."

"Yeah, a bunch of people left after you did," Lexi responded, glancing out the window at a spider slowly making its way down the glass. "Jeez, not another one. Damned things get bigger every day, I swear."

"Holy hell!" Sarah said, pulling every inch of her body away from the window.

"That thing's huge! It's like the size of my fist!"

"Yeah, they randomly started showing up around town a little while ago. Anyway, where's Big Bun? Wasn't he picking you up today?"

"He was *supposed* to, but you know my brother, he's all kinds of messed up."

"God, I ain't seen him in like, a week or so. He must've been setting up some crazy party plans for tonight. I bet he's at your place right now

"Maybe. When everyone gets here we'll go check. Where are they, anyway?"

"They should be showing up any time —
"

As if on cue, the small bell at the door rang exactly three times. The two turned towards the ringing, and their question was already answered.

There, standing in front of the closing glass door, were the three people they were waiting for. The tallest of the three, and the one standing in front, was Samuel, in his long white sweater, which had the words "Blood as red as my leaf" down one arm and "CANADA" down the other. The red shirt he wore beneath was stained with what the two girls could only assume was his morning coffee. They referred to him as K9 because, like a dog, he was always ready for the next plan.

Behind him was Tammy—or 'Hoot' as they called her, as she was the smart one of the group, like the wise owl. Her abnormally large round glasses covered nearly half her face, and were easily the first thing anyone noticed about her, with her burning red hair tied back as it was now. She was somewhat hiding behind Sam, anxiously looking at the new girl who had replaced their "Bunny."

Finally was Alex—Leo as they called him, his golden blond hair wrapped around his face like a bushy mane of the lion— standing at the side of Sam, showing just how much shorter he was than the tall K9.

Barely reaching the dog's shoulder, he stood proudly at his side, smiling and waving over to them. He was their newest friend, comparably. Sarah could clearly remember how surprised she was when he randomly introduced himself that day.

***

"Dammit, Bunny!" Lexi had said that strange summer evening.

It was unnaturally cold, even for Canada, and the girls had just spent all of their money buying Sarah a brand new hoodie as a going away present. Sarah remembered frantically telling the others not to bother, but they were adamant about it, knowing full well they wouldn't see their Bunny again for two years.

"I'm sorry, Kit," Sarah said, her long blonde hair flowing in the breeze. "I have to go to school. It's what I've always wanted!"

The wind blew past them, forcing their hair to lash at their faces like a run amok whip. Tammy held tightly to her glasses,

CRYPTID CHRONICLES: THE SPIDER

praying they didn't fly to the next country. Lexi's hat flipped off her head, but she caught it by the tips of her fingers.

"God," Lexi said, tightly pressing her knit beanie to her head. "What's with the weather lately?"

"Who knows?" Said Sarah, brushing her fingers through her now unkempt hair. "But I'm sure it'll be better soon enough."

"Not when you're gone," said Tammy, a whisper in the wind.

"I won't be gone forever!" Sarah said, wrapping her arms around the smaller girl. "Beside, we have a whole two months before then. We can party up a storm until I leave."

"Party?" A random boy said, stopping beside the three girls. "I looove to party!" He raised his fists in triumph.

"Sorry, buddy," Sarah said, trying to keep polite. "Just friends invited."

"Oh, come on. I could be a friend." He gave her a wink through the bangs of his long black hair. "Why don't you let me and

SCOTT FREER

my boys party with you girls? We could make it a 'banger.'" He gestured to the two larger boys behind him.

"I think we'll pass," responded Lexi, hardly thinking. "Besides, boys like you would have to try much harder to get girls like us." She winked and turned away, but stopped when she felt the firm hand on her shoulder.

"I don't think you're giving us a fair chance here, girl," the largest of the three said. His fake tanned skin immediately made her skin crawl, and the strange tribal tattoos along his arm didn't help in that regard.

"Like I said, no thank you." She tried to pull her shoulder, but his grip was tight.

"See, here's the thing," the first boy started. "My boys don't like to hear the answer 'no.' You understand, right?" He pulled back the flap of his vest to reveal the row of pocket knives neatly pocketed along the inside. "So I think you'll make the smart choice here."

30

Tammy's grip on her bag tightened, her eyes darting between the three huge, older boys. Sarah nervously twirled her finger through her hair, biting down on her red lip.

"I think," a voice said from behind the boys, "it should be *you* who makes the smart choice here, gentlemen."

"Hmm?" The tanned boy turned back to see the speaker, but found himself quickly tasting the bitter taste of the pavement.

Alex was standing behind him, rubbing his now reddened knuckles, waiting for the man to get back up, but he was down for the count. Lexi backed away, moving herself near the other girls. The one with the knives gestured to the third boy, who instantly started towards Alex.

Alex fiddled with a small silver lighter — this was the first time she saw it, sparkling in the moonlight. He flicked the flame to life, then snuffed it almost instantly.

The boy took a few steps towards him, but hesitated, eyes pinned to the small silver lighter in his hands. Alex noticed the boy's hesitation, and quickly stuffed the lighter back in his pocket.

"Sorry—habit. I won't use it as a weapon, if that's what you're worried about." He winked nonchalantly at the boy, whose face was growing redder and redder by the moment.

The boy lunged towards him, swinging his big, meaty fists back and forth through the air around Alex's face. Were it anyone else, he would've been on the ground in an instant, fighting against a larger man—in both height and width—with no measurable size of his own. But not Alex.

Everything the man threw Alex evaded with ease, sliding between the small spaces in the boy's punches. By the time the boy realized that everything he threw had missed, Alex was already inches away from his face.

"Boop," Alex said, poking the man's nose before spinning midair and kicking the side of his face. The man dropped like a brick, crashing to the ground with an enormous THUD.

"Goddammit!" The final boy said, pulling out a pair of long, wide switchblades. He flicked the blades open, twirling the handles through his fingers expertly.

Alex watched, slowly making his way towards the boy. His eyes were pinned to the man's, but he could easily see the flipping blades in the moonlight. The boy took a step towards him, then another, stopping the twirling blades to hold them backwards in his hands before darting towards Alex.

Alex planted his feet and raised his hand. The boy closed in. Fifteen feet. Ten feet. Five feet. The boy jumped at him, thrusting both blades down at Alex's neck. There was a brief moment—no longer than a second—when Sarah felt herself jumping out to help him, before seeing that strangely sinister grin peering through his otherwise calm face.

The blades crashed to the ground, clanging against the pavement before finally lying flat. One of the blades' tip cracked against the stones, sending a shard five feet away. The boy was quiet, leaning against Alex's closed fist planted firmly in his stomach. Alex felt the strange movements against his knuckles and pulled his fist back, allowing the man to fall to the ground, unconscious.

"You girls okay?" He asked, the genuine concern in his hazel eyes.

"Uhh…," Sarah stuttered.

"We're okay," Lexi finished, staring in awe at the small man.

Tammy nodded enthusiastically, her red face showing in the moonlight.

"Good. By the way, the name's Alex."

***

It wasn't long after that that he had made himself a frequent member of their group, and even gotten himself his own animal name to match. Samuel wasn't too happy at first, but eventually he realized that being the only boy in a group filled with girls wasn't the dream he thought it was.

Alex was the first to approach their table, followed almost immediately by the other two. Tammy was still hiding behind Sam's shoulder when they sat down across from her, while Alex sat happily beside her.

"Welcome back, 'Bunny'" Sam said from across the table.

"Yeah, yeah." She waved him off. "Get the edgy jokes out already, I deserve it."

"Well, you look so different!" Sam responded. "Like you took your former self and threw it away. Like 'I'm not cute anymore! I'm a dark lord!'"

"Like she ate Bunny," Tammy quietly added with a small giggle.

"Hey! Maybe we can give her a new name!" Lexi said, bouncing over at Tammy. "Hoot, what eats rabbits?"

"Um, well, lots of things, really. Some birds eat rabbits, like eagles."

"No birds, I hate birds," Sarah responded quickly.

"Well what about some kind of dog? Wolves and foxes eat rabbits all the time."

"Hey," said Sam, "We've already got a K9 here." He shoved his thumb into his chest proudly.

"Right, sorry Sammy." Tammy pushed up the bridge on her glasses.

"What about Snake?" Alex suggested. His voice instantly silenced the room. Something about his composure, and the finite tone in his voice, always brought attention to him in whatever conversation was going on. "She looks pretty edgy, and snakes eat bunnies."

"Snake...I like it!" Sarah said, wrapping an arm around Alex's shoulder. "Watch out, I might squeeze the life out of you."

Alex heaved a laugh and shoved her off.

"Snake! Wait, snakes don't eat cats, right?"

"I guess you'll have to find out, Kitty."

Sarah mimicked a snake's hiss as best she could, and they laughed out in mock terror. It took them a few moments to calm themselves down, all the memories of the six of them flooding back

"Hey, where's Big Bun?" Asked Lexi.

The group grew quiet suddenly. Sam's eyes dropped to the table, while Tammy was playing with the strings on her hoodie. Even Alex's normally strong look was down at his small silver lighter, flicking it back and forth uncomfortably.

"What is it?" Asked Sarah.

"Kit, you didn't hear?" Whispered Tammy.

"Hear what?" Answered Sarah, her tone growing more concerned.

"Sarah...," Sam started, pulling himself back quickly, the words catching in his throat.

"Erik went missing last week," finished Alex, clenching his hands together. Sarah could hear his knuckles cracking from the pressure. "Him and that one guy Joey, or whatever his name is. Last anyone saw them, they were somewhere around the Ghost Road."

Sarah was silent, fiddling with the broken heart pendant, which now seemed to be mocking her loss. Her grip tightened, and she could feel the sharp ridges digging like nails into the palm of her hand. She didn't release the grip, even as she felt the trickles of red begin dripping to the table beneath. Sam opened his mouth to speak, but Alex's raised hand stopped his words in his throat. The other girls sat in abject horror as the small droplets formed at the bottom of her hand and plunked into the tiny puddle they slowly formed. Sarah's eyes slowly raised themselves to meet Alex's at her side.

"Where?" Her cold words were filled with the venom of a snake that was out for blood.

***

Erik awoke in the dark, dank cave,

surrounded by the disgusting smell of rancid flesh and the bones of what he only assumed were this *thing's* past visitors. He could barely feel anything below his waist, save for the slight tingling sensation in the ends of his toes and along his bones. His stomach hurt severely, as if he had just been stabbed with a hot knife and no one had removed the blade. He tried moving himself, but struggled against the webbing that enveloped his body. The strength of the silk astounded him as he pushed with all his might, to no avail. He dropped his head back against the hard stone behind him, breathing out the heavy, exhausted air. He could almost hear it, the sound of his sister's plane landing just a few miles away from the city. He pressed his fingers against the silver heart beneath the wrappings.

The heart! He thought to himself, gripping tightly on the half-heart pendant. He pressed it firmly against the web-like wrapping and began sawing it back and forth. Slowly he cut through the tightly knit strands one by one.

A sudden skittering sound echoed through the tunnel—he could hear her closing towards the cave. He furiously sawed the webbing, severing it strand by strand. He felt the tearing like a grinding sound in his ears, but eventually the wrapped webbing ripped just enough for him to pull himself out.

Erik's legs were still fairly numb, but he knew he didn't have the time to wait for their feeling to return. He pulled himself out the freshly made hole in the webbing and onto the hard stone ground of the cave.

The skittering sound grew louder and louder as she approached him. Each sharpened spear-like leg stabbing down into the rock beneath her feet resonated like an echo through the tunnels. He could hear her breathing, a hissing sound like a snake preparing a strike—only much, much louder. He pulled himself along the ground, his numb legs dragging behind him. The exhaustion of the night had run him dry, and nearly destroyed his muscles. Yet with what little strength he had, he dragged his nearly lifeless body across the rough, cave floor and threw himself behind a large spire. The crash brought the pain in his stomach to a new high, and he gripped tightly on his abdomen and held back the urge to vomit.

He rested to catch his breath, and he heard her. A long, thin, spiny leg shot near him, barely a foot away from where he was sitting at the other end of the spire. He could see each individual silver hair springing out from the leg like a thorn on a rose. He could almost smell the horrid slimy secretions that poured out of her mouth.

The strange sound came—he heard it occasionally whenever he was hiding from her. It almost sounded like some kind of fruit being crushed beneath someone's foot. He could see her head just over the spire, the silver hair poured out like a waterfall down her back. He heard the small gasp, then the angry hissing came back. It sounded like a dog whistle, piercing his ears. He gripped at the sides of his head, desperately wanting to scream out in pain. He barely found the willpower to bite his tongue, holding back the pitiful scream.

The hissing stopped, and the strange sound burst again. The leg shot back as she scurried back through the tunnels towards that hellish game store. He pulled himself up on the spire. The feeling in his legs seemed to be returning. He noticed that the stubbed wound where his ankle once had been was healed over. He pressed it against the ground; there was no pain, save for the sharp rocks digging into his flesh.

He made his way slowly around the spire, checking for that evil witch or any of her "precious" children. He didn't see any signs of the terror inducing monsters, only the strange runes and symbols carved along the walls of the tunnels. He slowly made his way up the tunnel, propping himself against the wall when he felt the exhaustion taking hold of him again. His vision blurred, and his muscles weakened. He gripped tightly on the small wound on his stomach under his ripped and bloodied shirt, and pressed forward.

He turned the first corner slowly, checking for any creatures on the hunt. There were a few rats and other unsavory pests, but he knew they were of no worry to him. The rancid smell grew closer and closer as he made his way down what he hoped was the correct tunnel, listening to the consistent chittering all through the halls. The millions of tiny knives digging into the earth each time one of those horrid beasts took a step would haunt his mind forever, he knew.

He felt one of the strange characters on the wall; it looked similar to a star, with a few minor changes in details. If he weren't so exhausted, he could've sworn that it was glowing green.

The chittering grew louder now, and he heard something growing closer. He hurried into the nearest cave and threw himself into a break in the rocks, his breathing deep and heavy. He slowed his heart as best he could, but its beat was still vicious in his chest. The smell was revolting now—had he not known better, he would've thought he'd jumped into the garbage bin of a disgusting restaurant. He closed his eyes tight, listening.

The chittering stopped outside the cave he was in—he could practically hear them breathing. He didn't dare open his eyes—their giant, white, hairy bodies would've made him scream to the high heavens. His fear of spiders was the entire reason that idiot Joey had dragged him into this old shop in the first place.

Joey…, he thought. His heart sank deep. He could only hope his friend was okay, even with the almost certain knowledge that he wasn't.

He heard the chittering drift off down

the tunnel as the two giant monsters went on their way. Erik opened his eyes, and his urge to scream returned. He barely held his tongue — he could feel the sounds making their way up his throat and pushing against his lips, refusing to be held in.

The horrific site in front of him, the terrifying scene that would haunt his days forever, was of his own best friend, Joey, laying on the cold, rocky floor, staring blankly up at him, with his ribcage ripped open from the inside.

Erik wanted to scream as loud as possible but forced every muscle he had into holding that force down. With his back flush against the wall, and eyes pinned to the man he once called his friend, he tightened his muscles and forced himself to keep whatever still filled his stomach from forcing it's way up his throat and all over the rocky cavern ground. Joey's body was so strangely attacked, so bizarrely and horrifically mutilated, that even the

SCOTT FREER

worst things in Erik's imagination couldn't accurately explain the horrific scene splayed out before his eyes. Erik pulled himself up — with difficulty — and edged his way around his dead friend. Only now did he notice the many other bodies lining the walls of the cave. Each of them resembled one of the missing posters — at least they would have had they not been so mangled and torn away. Erik pressed himself to move out of the cave and find his way out. He heard the chittering down the tunnel from which he had come, so he turned down the other and began his journey out.

THE SEARCH

The thunderous roar of the engine echoed in the empty night. Pale moonlight illuminated the beaten down roads and shone off the shattered windows in each of the deserted buildings along the Ghost Road. The once busy and bustling Jackson Street, filled with shops and homes which stretched from one end of town to the other, was now a silent ghost town on the edge of reality. Infestations, robberies, and a hundred other horrible issues had caused any who once lived or resided in these decrepit buildings to flee to somewhere safe. Sarah stared up through the broken windows into the dark, empty rooms, wondering what kind of people had lived there, and what exactly caused them to flee so suddenly.

Lexi nervously tightened her grip on the wheel. The silver rings on her fingers buried themselves into her flesh, but she couldn't care. She found herself constantly shooting her eyes between the buildings and the road in front of her, and her best friend sat beside her as they looked for her missing brother. In the back of the car Tammy was fiddling with her tablet, searching desperately for any news about those who had gone missing these past few weeks, specifically for a blue pickup truck matching his plates.

RIIING RIIING

Sarah reached into her pocket, pulling out the bright red phone. She answered, activating the speaker so the rest could hear.

"Sarah, we've been searching for hours." Sam's exhausted voice resounded in the car. "Can we call it a night? We'll start again first thing in the morning, I promise."

"Not until we find some kind of clue," Sarah said, eyes still staring out the window at every detail in the houses and old stores along the road. "He's my brother, and we're not stopping for anything."

"Snake...." Lexi's soft words were met with a dull silence.

"Meet us at the old game store. We'll discuss it there." Alex's finite tone made it clear that this wasn't a request.

"Fine." Sarah hung the phone up, tossing it down at her side.

"Snakey." Lexi placed a hand on her friend's shoulder. "You know we're trying to help, right?"

"Obviously." Sarah refused to take her eyes away from the window.

"And you know we'd do anything for you, right?"

"I know that."

"Erik's been missing for a while now." Lexi made her tone as soft as possible. "I mean, I haven't seen him in a while. So maybe we should take a small break, and tackle it first thing tomorrow."

"You can 'take a break.'" Sarah's stern tone was foreign to her. Even when they were kids, arguments were almost never serious, with Sarah's chipper, high-pitched voice. "For all I know my brother's dead in a ditch somewhere."

"You can't think that," Tammy said quietly from the back seat. "I'm sure he's okay. Maybe he…." She searched for an answer, some calming explanation, but she drew nothing but a blank.

"Exactly," Sarah responded. "Which is why I can't…."

She saw the tear in her reflection before she ever felt it trickle down her face. She quickly wiped it away before the others could notice.

They drove past several decrepit houses before they finally arrived in the empty parking lot of the old Mark's Game-

and-Stop. The only car for miles that they could see was the clean orange sport's car that belonged to Alex's older brother. The moonlight bounced off the flaming details along the side, making an almost realistic-looking fire across the door. Samuel was propped up against the passenger's side door, barely seeming to keep himself awake. Alex sat on the hood, flicking his lighter on and off, watching the flame flicker out then burst back to life in an instant. His eyes met Sarah's as he looked up at the three girls approaching them from across the lot.

"What is it?" Sarah asked, in a more demanding tone than she had meant.

"Relax, Sarah." The words left Samuel's mouth before he realized what had happened.

"Relax? Relax?!" Sarah stomped her way towards him, finding herself growing angrier with each consecutive step. "You expect me to relax and chill out when my brother might be dead in a ditch somewhere?!

Or bloodied and beaten in an alley, barely clinging to life?! Don't tell me to relax Sam!"

Unknowingly, she raised a fist to strike, but found it stopping suddenly when she tried to throw it forward. She looked over her shoulder; Alex's hand was wrapped tightly around her wrist, eying her down while his other hand flicked the lighter shut again. She yanked her arm back and Alex let go, sending her back a few feet, nearly onto the ground. He stepped between the two, barely meeting Samuel's chest. Even he was shaking behind the smaller man.

"Sarah," Alex said, unblinking, and unwavering. "K9's taking the girls home. Just looking at them I can tell they're ready to drop. Tammy's barely keeping her eyes open as it is, and Lexi had been busting ass at work before this."

"Well, busting ass is a bit of an exaggeration," Lexi responded, a slight chuckle in her voice.

"So you're just giving up?" Said Sarah,

taking a step towards Alex. "What if it was your brother? What if he went missing? Would you want us to give up? Would we even give up at all?"

"We're not giving up, Sarah," Samuel responded.

"No, you're going home because you're a bit 'tired.' Is that what it is?"

"Six hours of looking around the same place, Sarah." Sam's tone was growing cold. "Yes, I'm exhausted from staring at the same damn trees and broken down buildings looking for a dead man!"

Sam tried to stop the words, but they had already left. The silence was deafening in their ears, and Sarah's cold, icy look was like needles in his eyes. Alex's grip tightened on the lighter, uncomfortably feeling for the flint-wheel. He flicked it aflame again, leaving the fire dancing in the silence.

"I…. I didn't mean…." Sam tried futilely to take his words back, but in her eyes he could see it wasn't possible.

"Get out," she muttered, eyes still pinned to his. He could see tears forming in the corners of her eyes.

"Kit, let K9 Drive you guys home." Alex said, snuffing the flame. "Sarah and I will keep looking around for a bit."

Sarah's eyes snapped down to meet his own. The same icy stare stabbed into his rough hazel eyes. The two locked unwavering eyes for a moment—which felt like an hour to both of them—before Sam took his cue to make his way around them. He whispered something to the other two girls, then pulled them away towards Lexi's father's van. The three of them waved to the two of them, and though they still locked eyes, Alex waved back as the black van pulled out of the lot and moved down the road into town.

Only after the bright red taillights had drifted off into the distance, turning the corner down Main Street, did Alex finally end their staring contest, turning back towards his older brother's sports car. He pulled open the driver's door and sat himself down. He flicked the key to the side and the powerful roar of the engine sprung to life, shining bright headlights on the furious face of his friend, who made her way to the passenger's door. She sat silently next to Alex, clicking her seatbelt and gluing her eyes to the window.

At a snail's pace they made their way through the empty, dying Ghost Street, inspecting each and every detail as they went. Their drive was silent, save for the few instances when either one spotted something they thought important, even though it always turned out to be nothing. Stopping every time they found some obscure detail was growing irritating to the two of them. Alex could easily see Sarah's exhaustion, despite how vigorously she was hiding it.

Alex pulled over, parking the car at the side of the road next to the same game-and-stop from which their search had started. He stared out at the brush next to the road curiously. The small group of trees and bushes seemed almost fabricated to his eyes. He rubbed his temples, feeling the deep exhaustion. He considered searching through the trees, but stopped, considering it just a trick of the light, or perhaps his exhaustion. The exasperated sigh from his side caught his attention, pulling his sight.

"Look at yourself," he said, keeping his voice as tender as possible. "You're ready to collapse. Let's call it a night and grab everyone in the morning."

She silently stared out the window, refusing to answer.

"No one's giving up, Snake. Running ourselves ragged this late at night isn't going to help. It's only going to make it more difficult in the morning—"

"I'm sorry...," she said, wiping the tears forming in her eyes. "I shouldn't have screamed at you guys earlier."

56

"It's your brother, no one blames you."

Sarah gripped the handle and opened her door, leaving it hanging as she took a seat on the hood of the car. Alex sat for a moment, allowing her a time of solitude, before opening his own door to sit at her side.

"You know we'll find him," whispered Alex, trying not to overwhelm her.

"What makes you say that?" She asked, staring off down the empty road.

"It's a small town." He shrugged his shoulders. "How far could he go?"

"To be honest, I'd rather not think how far he could go."

"You need to stop thinking like—" He cut himself short, noticing a glinting reflection out of the corner of his eyes.

"What?" Inquired Sarah, looking in the direction he was staring. "What?" She asked again.

He quickly jogged over to the curb at the other side of the road, seeing the moonlight shining off the piece of metal. He picked it up and flipped it over.

"Sarah, what was Erik's plate?"

"XEDJ-674, why?"

There was an audible gasp that came from Alex. He turned to show her the sheet of metal he'd found. It was a license plate, with the code XEDJ-674.

Sarah ran over and grabbed the plate from his hands. It was her brother's plate. Her head shot in every direction looking for that hideous blue pickup, but she couldn't see it anywhere. She started around the game-and-stop, looking for the truck, which was suddenly seeming more beautiful by the minute.

Alex took a moment to look around as well, searching along the road for any sign of the truck. "Why would he take off the plate...?" He whispered to himself.

He approached his own car, flicking his lighter on and off as he went. The metal bent slightly beneath him as he dropped his rear against the hood. His mind was racing with a thousand questions, yet no answers. He turned towards the brush, the strikingly unnatural brush.

Sarah threw the plate viciously against the brick wall of the game-and-stop. Clenching her fingers into a tight fist, she dropped to her knees. The truck was nowhere to be seen. She felt almost close enough to hear him calling to her. The pendant — that stupid little pendant — felt so close she could almost touch it. She saw the droplets crash against the ground before she ever felt them form in her eyes. In the silence of the moonlit night each tiny splash of tears breaking against the broken asphalt beneath her resounded in her head a thousand times louder, like a rockslide crashing into the ocean.

Alex approached the strangely colored brush, gripping tightly on his silver lighter. The moonlight bounced synthetically off the bright emerald leaves, like plastic. He

SCOTT FREER

gripped a handful of the wide, full leaves,
but pulled his hand back almost instantly.
He rubbed one between his fingers curiously.
They felt oddly rough, like fine sandpaper.
He pulled back, expecting the stem to snap
with relative ease, but it held strong against
his pull. He pulled a bit harder, yet the stem
still pulled back. Finally, with one hard
yank, the stem cracked and broke with a
loud snap. Alex nearly toppled back from
the sudden break, barely gaining his footing
on the uneven ground.

Sarah pushed herself back to her feet,
slowly approaching the thin metal license.
The corner had been chipped off from the
force of impact. She picked up the shard and
twirled it a bit in her fingers curiously. The
way the moonlight bounced hypnotized her,
reminding her of the moment her brother
first bought the horrendous blue truck.

Something caught her eye; a small,
white speck she saw just out the corner of
her eye, moving across the crumbling black

ground. She darted her eyes towards it out of instinct: a large white spider, about the size of her thumb, was crawling towards the building. She dropped the shard and barely contained the scream that begged to be released. The spider stopped briefly at the base of the wall, staring back at the enormous, strange creature, before crawling through a small, barely noticeable opening in the ground. Sarah felt her spine shake uncomfortably, sending shivers through every bone and every nerve in her body.

"I hate spiders...," she whispered to herself, wrapping her arms around her body.

Alex fiddled with the leaf, staring curiously at the rest of the brush. The small tear he'd made in the leaf made it clear to him that it was not a natural leaf. The small twine remnants that were left between the two pieces were a clear sign that it wasn't as it seemed. His eyes were eventually brought to the place that this leaf was torn from;

in the small, barely noticeable space left behind, he saw some small sheen coming from within. The leaf fell from his fingers as he reached towards the brush, grabbing a handful of the fake leaves and pulling back.

Like a wall with no foundation, the brush began to topple towards him. He saw the flat world of leaves tumbling at him and jumped back out of the way, narrowly avoiding the oncoming crash. The wall of leaves burst against the ground with a whap, the air nearly sending his open jacket flying from his body. He stared down at the "brush" of leaves. The intertwining material was interesting to him, most notably that it was not natural, nor were there any leaves on the "back" side of the brush. He looked up at the place where the wall once was. The sharp intake of breath nearly made him choke.

Sarah approached the small hole in the ground. She crouched near it, pulling out her phone and activating the flashlight. The inside of the hole was abnormally deep—she couldn't see anything at the bottom, like a pipe which went on forever. It felt strange to her, like it couldn't have formed naturally, or by the force of time passing over this broken and beaten landscape. Nowhere around the hole were there any signs of breaking asphalt, not for a few feet in any direction. Not that the hole was a rough, cracked creation. She didn't consider herself any sort of trade expert, but even to her the hole seemed intentionally made, like it were made with a very long drill. She dropped the shard of metal through the hole. It silently fell for a moment before crashing slightly against the side of the hole. Sarah heard it crack and smack against the sides lightly for a moment before the sound faded into silence.

"Sarah!" She heard Alex shout front the other side of the building. "Get over here!"

She jumped to her feet, grabbing the license plate, and ran towards where she had left Alex and his car. When she turned the corner, stuffing her phone back in her pocket, she saw Alex tearing apart a group of bushes, which all seemed slightly larger to her than the average bush did. She intended on yelling at him for destroying what little nature still resided in this deserted hell, until she saw that horrendous blue shine coming from between the bushes.

"It's—" Her voice cut out as the final wall of leaves dropped in front of them.

"You were right," Alex said, placing a hand on her shoulder. "It is hideous."

Sarah stared blankly at the blue truck crashed against the old oak tree. The dented metal and scratched trunk brought horrific images to her mind. She took a step forward, but stopped short, horrified at the thought of what she might find. Alex laid a hand on her shoulder and urged her forward, smiling with faded hope. The license fit snuggly back on the bumper of the truck. Sarah felt an air of comfort when she saw the truck she remembered wearing its license plate. Something akin to nostalgia washed over her face, but drained just as quickly as she remembered the dents and scars all along the side.

Sarah stood, knowing where she wanted to search first. She took another step forward, then a third. The back window was shattered, with remnants of the glass on both the inside and outside of the truck. The shard of glass inches from slicing her neck open wasn't nearly as frightening as the state she found the interior in.

The seat itself was clawed and scratched to hell. The tearing and ripped leather revealed the springs and material inside the seat, making it look almost like an autopsy of the vehicle. Finally, floating like a silk cloud, was an abnormally large spider's web. The silky strands were very thick, and she wondered what kind of spider could do that. As it floated around, bouncing in the moonlight, Sarah noticed the slight blue luminescent glow coming off it. It reminded her of the way moonlight bounced off the blue ocean. She wondered what kind of animal had broken in, but realized she didn't want to know.

The thought had finally come over her, knowing what she needed to do, and what she wished she didn't have to. Her hand gripped the driver's door handle, but didn't pull it open immediately. No matter how much she tried to force her hand to pull the latch open, her nerves refused to release the tight grip they had over her. She looked back over her shoulder at Alex, and he took a few steps towards her. His calm smile loosened her tense muscles and allowed her to finally pull the handle back.

The door opened rather easily, considering the bent metal and scratched edges along the opening. Her arm retracted slowly, allowing her to watch through the crack as the door inched open. Sarah wasn't sure what she expected. Perhaps she was expecting to see the body of her brother hunched over the dashboard or crashed through the window — perhaps she expected to see the body of that boy Joey he was always hanging out with. Regardless of what Sarah was hoping or dreading to see when the door finally creaked open, what she was met with hadn't even crossed her mind.

The interior of the driver's side was nearly untouched, save for a few remnants of glass from the windshield crashing into the tree, and a couple of indentations from that same crash. Other than those few markings, it almost seemed like no one had been in the car when it crashed. The driver's seat was nearly unmarked, and the only sign that her brother had been in the truck within the last few weeks was the stained wooden pocket knife sitting in the passenger's seat. Sarah reached over the seat for the knife, palmed it, and flicked the blade out with the small latch. The satisfying sound sent a chill down

SCOTT FREER

her spine. She eyed the blade, inspecting it for any dents or marks of use, then closed the knife again and started back. Something caught her eye: a small keychain she had bought her brother for his birthday three years before, jangling behind the wheel. She reached in and pulled the small star-shaped key ring from the ignition and fiddled with the keys in the palm of her hand.

Suddenly she stopped, noticing the white shape, almost the size of her fist sitting on the dashboard. Instinctively, Sarah found her hand reaching out towards it. Her finger's shook, and her bones chilled with each inch she moved closer. Her fingertip barely grazed the shape's hairy white exterior before it jumped to life right in front of her eyes.

The spider jumped out the door and scurried past Sarah, which sent shivers down her spine and made a loud, high pitched scream burst out from the deepest recesses of her heart. She threw herself at the hood of the car and watched the small white shape make its way towards Alex. Alex jolted back at her scream, barely understanding what had just happened until he saw the same small white shape closing in on him. With his feet planted firmly in place, and his eyes fixed to the white arachnid, he watched until it was just in front of him, then raised and dropped his foot on top of it. The unnerving crunch beneath his foot—like wood splitting under intense pressure—made his heart skip a beat.

Sarah started towards him, but stopped at a sudden sound—a sudden loud hissing sound, like a hushed whisper in the air, but clearly loud enough to echo. Sarah slowly approached Alex, who was frantically looking around the ground for the snake or animal that had made that sound.

"You heard that too, right?" He asked her.

"The hissing?" She replied, "Yeah, it sounded like a snake, probably pretty close, too."

"Right." The two made their way towards the sport's car. "Guess he wasn't in there?"

"No," she responded, eyes staring down at the pocket knife. "It looked like he hadn't been there in a couple of days at least."

"I wonder...." Alex looked back at the truck, considering the method with which it had crashed. In his mind's eye he came up with several scenes, and considered which to be the most likely, or which to be the best place to start investigating. "Maybe he was running from something, and crashed?" He whispered, more to himself than anyone else.

"Running?"

"Well, why else would the license plate have been missing?" He gestured to the plate Sarah had attached to the back of the car. "If he was running from something and accidentally crashed, they'd probably want to keep him, or anyone else for that matter, from finding the car. So they took the license plate, and covered the car in leaves."

"I mean, I suppose, but that's a pretty heavy long shot," Sarah responded. "Besides, what would he be running from?"

"I don't know." Alex pointed towards the game-and-stop. "But if I were hiding from something, an old, abandoned game store wouldn't be a bad place to hide."

"You think he's hiding in there?"

"Maybe not, but it's a start." Alex pulled out his phone, flicking the screen on, "Look, it's past midnight. What do you say we grab the others in the morning and start looking through the buildings? We'll start with the game-and-stop together, then split up if he's not there. Fair?"

Sarah felt herself growing exhausted from the hours of searching. "We found the car—I suppose we can do more in the morning. Fine…."

Alex placed a hand on her shoulder, looking her in the eyes. "Look, if he's anywhere around here, we'll find him." He smiled a friendly grin. "We can't lose our Big Bun!"

Sarah grinned to herself, wondering how he ever got that name. "Fine, let's go."

Alex pulled his keys from his pocket and opened the passenger side door, helping Sarah in. She sat quietly, finally feeling just how tired she really was, while he made his way around to his side. He sat next to her, placing his key in the ignition but not turning it.

"You got a place to stay tonight?" He asked.

"I was gonna go home," she said. "But it'd be pretty weird without him there."

"Want to stay over for the night?" He asked, trying his best to keep his face from reddening.

"Your brother won't mind?"

"He's out for the night, won't be back until tomorrow night."

"Sure, sounds like a plan." She smiled

back at him as he turned the key and drove off into the night.

***

PLINK PLINK PLINK

The droplets of water swelled and bloated before plunging from the stalactites hanging from the ceiling of the dark, dank tunnel. Each crash echoed violently in Erik's ears, ringing in his mind like a thousand church bells. In the distance he could still barely hear the chittering and skittering of thousands of tiny, dagger-like legs slashing and stabbing at the rough earthy floor in search of him.

The blurry image of the long, dark tunnel shook and wavered in and out of existence. Erik rubbed his eyes, stumbling for a moment and nearly toppling over to the floor. He wiped the sweat from his brow, wincing at the stinging pain across all the scrapes and cuts he'd accumulated over his time in this hell. The rotting smell and thick, disgusting air made him retch and

73

heave. The clenching pain in his stomach nearly brought him to his knees—and he barely had the strength to push himself forward tooth and nail. He gritted his teeth and propped himself against the wall for support, dragging his arm along the sharp, rocky surface.

His slow, heavy footsteps echoed in the wide tunnel. Each step took longer than the last, and felt more and more like his final step in this world. His stump leg crashed uncomfortably against the uneven ground, making his limping walk more and more difficult with each continuous step.

Suddenly his stump leg slipped on something wet and sent him tumbling down. He crashed against the floor, whacking the side of his head on a hard patch of dirt, just barely missing the sharpened rock a couple of inches in front of his eyes.

He rubbed his fresh wound, wiping the dirt from his head—along with the small stain of blood—and pushed himself up on his knees. He looked back at the small green stain where he had slipped. The smell and consistency were all too familiar to him at this point. He was only happy that the venomous slime was already dried and worn to the point of safety, even if it was still a bit slippery under his step.

He stayed there a moment, kneeling to catch his breath. He fiddled with the silver pendant around his neck, pressing a finger against the jagged, worn-down edge thoughtfully. He wondered if Sarah was still wearing hers, wherever she was.

Suddenly something caught his eye, just for a brief second, then it vanished from sight—a small white speck on the wall. He rubbed his eyes and looked again, but it was already gone. He heard the faint, almost inaudible scratching of nails against rock drifting into the distance.

He quickly pulled himself to his feet, nearly toppling back down from the sudden rush of fear, and pushed himself forward as quickly as his limp, borderline lifeless body would take him. He walked in silence for a moment before the sudden hissing sound arose, shrieking like an angry spirit past his ears, ringing them like a bell. He clenched his teeth, holding back the urge to cry out in pain. The hissing went on for more than a moment before stopping. And when it did stop, Erik only had a moment of relief before he heard another, equally terrifying sound. He caught his breath, loosening his grip on the pendant—after realizing how deep the indentations from the jagged edge were—for no more than a second before hearing the thousands upon thousands of convulsive, frantic ticking steps rapidly approaching. What was worse was that they weren't all the light steps of the smaller babies. Some of the steps were much, much heavier.

He stared up the tunnel as quickly as possible, but soon realized his attempts were futile. His feet wouldn't take him much farther, his legs being sapped of what little energy he had left, and it took everything he had to prevent them from crumbling beneath him. He pressed on, praying to anything that might possibly hear him that he might make it out in time, before looking over his shoulder to see all the different red, glowing eyes down the tunnel, spiraling through the darkness, rapidly approaching him.

THE TRUTH

Sarah heaved a heavy yawn as she turned the keys, locking the small wooden door. She stuck her finger through the silver keyring and began twirling the keys around as she made her way across the porch.

Alex was leaning against the hood of his brother's car talking on the phone. The tin metal bent slightly under his weight. Sarah quietly approached the passenger's side door, crouching behind it, ready to pounce as soon as Alex's phone call had finished. There was something in his voice, however, that made her hesitate and listen more intently.

"Yes, ma'am," he began. "It'll be done tonight, I'll see to it myself. Of course it's been difficult without Allison and Emily, but I've managed so far. Yes, ma'am, the office?" Alex raised to his feet, popping the metal back to its original shape. "What about it? Yes, I'll be sure to find it first. I'll call you tonight with my findings once it's finished. The boy? He's top priority in the mission, of course, but it may already be too late." He was silent for a moment, listening intently to whoever was on the other end. He gritted his teeth and clenched his hand into a tightly closed fist. "Yes, ma'am, of course. The mission comes first. Six out." He clicked the phone shut and shoved it back into his pocket.

"So who was that?" Sarah exclaimed, pouncing suddenly to surprise him.

"Jesus, Sarah!" Alex crashed to the ground, "Could've given me a heart attack!"

"Sorry," Sarah said with mock appeal.

"So who was on the phone?"

"What?" Alex responded, wiping down the back of his jeans.

"That woman. You kept saying 'ma'am,' a bunch so she must be important." Sarah crossed her arms

"Oh, that was just my little cousin." Alex said, patting himself on his now sore bottom. She loves playing secret agents whenever I come over, so I gave her my personal number. Now we can play secret agents whenever!" he said with false excitement. "Gets kind of annoying after a while though."

"Yeah, family can get annoying every once in a while…." Sarah's eyes suddenly downcast at her shoes.

She opened the door and flopped down into the passenger's seat, pulling the door shut behind her. Her hair, she could see in the reflection of the mirror, was frizzy and unkempt. She tried her best to fix it, but by the time Alex's door began slowly opening, she had already given up and shoved the mirror back up into the roof.

Alex sat down and shoved the keys in the ignition. He glanced briefly at her, smiling, then turned the keys and started off towards the Ghost Street.

"So," Sarah started, somehow uncomfortable with the situation. "We start with Mark's, and if he's not there, we split up and check the other buildings."

"Sounds like a plan," Alex said, not taking his eyes off the road. "There's only so many buildings, and he's gotta be somewhere. If not, we'll ask around the other side of town. Either way, we'll find him." He threw her a quick grin and turned the corner.

"How can you be so sure? It's been a week—he could've made it to God knows where by now."

"Well, we found his truck crashed against a tree, so he's not getting too far without that." He turned the corner, making his way down Melvin Drive.

"And if he found a new car?" Sarah

asked.

"Then someone would've seen him." Alex pulled the car through a lot, then turned onto Jackson—the Ghost Street. "Nevertheless, you can bet we'll know more by the end of today."

He pulled into the game-and-stop parking lot where two other cars were parked. Lexi's black van was parked right beside the building, close enough that she was able to lay back on the hood of the van with her feet pressed firmly against the red brick wall of the game-and-stop. She was playing around on her phone nonchalantly while she waited for the others to arrive, with her legs jiggling uncomfortably against the wall. Beside the van, Tammy was crouching up against the back door, staring down at her tablet intensely. Sarah could only imagine what she was doing on there, but if she were able to see, she would only see her reading a fantasy novella about monsters and mythology.

At the other end of the parking lot was a small blue two-door sedan. It was well-worn, but it seemed like a nice little car, considering the condition. In front of it was Samuel, leaning against the front bumper of the car, careful not to damage it any further than it already was. He tossed his keys in the air and caught them on their way down, over and over again. In his mouth appeared to be some sort of cigarette—although, if you asked him about it, he'd probably say it was something else. He was the first to notice the bright orange sports car rolling in from the streets, shoving his keys in his pocket and standing to meet them. He called something out to the others, who followed suit.

Alex turned the keys and pulled them from the ignition. He went to open his door, but stopped suddenly, noticing Sarah's downcast stare at her fingers, fiddling with the small, star-shaped keyring.

"What's wrong?" He asked, knowing full well what the answer would be.

"I'm going to have to apologize to everyone now, aren't I?" Sarah's eyes were full of regret, Alex noticed, as she turned towards him.

"Yeah...," he answered. "We have to clear the air around here, and you *did* almost punch K9 in the face." He gave her a smirk. "That's a fight I would've watched under different circumstances."

"Oh really? Who do you think would win?"

"Well, put a bunny against a dog and see what happens." He chuckled as the words left his mouth.

"A *snake,*" Sarah corrected him, emphasizing it with a hiss.

Alex laughed for a moment before pushing his door open and hopping out of the car. The door crashed shut before Alex tapped on the window, gesturing for Sarah to hop out. She pushed her door open as well, but hesitated for a moment, scratched at the back of her head uncomfortably, and stepped out of the car, closing the door behind her. There was a loud click and Alex shoved the keys back into his pocket, pulling out his lighter with the other hand. He flicked the top open and fiddled with the wheel until the flame sparked to life.

Sarah anxiously approached the others. Samuel had just reached Lexi's van by the time she shut her door. Lexi glanced over with a smile and a small wave. Sarah waved back awkwardly, noticing that her own nervous look was mirrored in Samuel's face as he waved.

"Glad we all made it," Sam said, his voice tense. "Hey guys."

"Hey, K9," Alex said, bumping his fist against Samuel's. "How're you doing, girls?"

"A bit tired," Lexi responded, exaggerating a loud stretch. "But I'm all right."

"I'm fine," Tammy responded quietly, darting her eyes between Sam and Sarah.

85

Sarah quietly stood behind Alex, rubbing her shoulders as if she was freezing in the warm summer air. Alex turned around to see her, gesturing her forward. She walked to his side, and only proceeded after he shoved her forward with his shoulder.

"Right—" she started.

"Hey, Sarah?" Samuel interrupted.

"Hmm?" Sarah's surprised look must've read on her face, and Samuel pulled back a bit.

"Oh, I just wanted to apologize for last night," he said, hardly able to look her in the eye. "It was kind of selfish for me to back out just because I was a bit tired—it *is* your brother, after all. So I just wanted to say I'm sorry."

"You're kidding," Sarah said, the mild hint of a smile etched in her face.

"What?" Samuel looked at her, worried she was still upset. He jumped back again as she burst out laughing.

"I...I was...." She could barely contain

the anxious laughter. "I was going to apologize to you guys!"

Samuel let a bit of a smile leak through, and eventually he, along with the others, started laughing alongside her. It was a strange moment that none of them really understood, laughing during such a dark moment before starting the search for the missing, possibly dead, Erik.

"I guess that means we're cool?" Asked Samuel as the laugher slowly faded.

"As long as you're cool with it, I am too," Sarah responded, "That goes for you girls too. I'm sorry I made you guys work so hard at this."

"We're totally okay with it!" Lexi said, hopping down from the hood, nearly onto her face.

"Well, you cut into my reading time," Tammy whispered, more to herself than to the others. "But I suppose we're all coolio." She smiled up at her.

"That's great," Sarah said, wiping the

tear from the corner of her eye, hoping no one noticed. "And hey," she turned to Samuel, "next time I raise the fist it'll be in good sport!"

"You think you could take the K9?" He said, crossing his arms defiantly.

"I'm not that little girl you used to know. Maybe we'll find out some day." She winked slyly at him.

"All right, ladies," Alex said, stepping between them. "We'll burn that bridge when we get to it, but for now can we move on?" He gestured to the game-and-stop.

The broken and beaten down red brick building stared down at them like a monolithic statue. The cracking bricks, chipped stones and gashed innards of the walls only now came to light as they stared up at the building in which their friend may, in fact, be laying alone, dying. The silent morning air seemed almost ominous. The only sound they could hear was the anxious clicking of Alex's silver lighter.

Sarah was the first to move, reaching out to open the rusted iron door, but hesitated. The others looked on at her fearful look, which felt more and more genuine than it had at first.

"What if he's in there…?" Sarah's voice was very quiet, nearly inaudible. "What if he's in there, and he's hurt? What if he was running from someone, and they caught him? What if they're in there with him?"

"Sarah, we can't know anything until we open that door."

Alex's firm voice set her mind at rest as best it could, though the thoughts still picked and prodded at her arm as she reached for the handle.

The coarse, rusty steel dug intensely into all of her fingers, lining a deep groove across each one, and a large, heavy, orange rut in her palm for each and every bit of rust that spiked out like a nail. She tried to twist the handle, but the rusty innards of the door must have been destroyed more than she imagined. She grabbed at it with both hands, jerking the handle left, then right, then left, trying to loosen the small metal pieces stuck together by years of hardship.

Eventually the handle gave way, sliding suddenly to the side, sending the door open with a crash. The sudden pull of the door handle flying open left a large bloody scar across the palm of Sarah's right hand. She hardly noticed it, the blood forming large, bulbous droplets at the tip of her fingers before falling to the ground with a splash.

"Snake, your hand!" Lexi said, running to the back of the large black van her father had loaned her for the day. She pulled out a small white box with a large red cross on it, and flung open the top.

Sarah peeked inside, and saw not only the average Band-Aids, gauze pads, and alcohol swabs, but several other items. The most intriguing to her was the black heavy-duty police flashlight sitting at the side of the box, beside a flare-torch and an abnormally long roll of gauze, which easily could've wrapped fully around any of them.

"Here, wipe it down with this," Lexi said, handing her a brown bottle with a squirt nozzle on top. Sarah sprayed a small spritz on the open cut along her lifeline. Her muscles tensed as the stinging pain shot through her hand, firing towards the tips of her fingers like lightning. She felt her teeth grit together, holding back the small yelp that wanted to escape her lungs. Lexi handed her a small white gauze pad, and Sarah rubbed thoroughly in the increasingly reddening wound.

"Leo, grab the gauze wrap and unroll enough to wrap her hand."

"The what?" Asked Leo.

"That! The big white wrap in the corner!"

"Oh...," Alex muttered, reaching in to grab the wrap. He placed a bit under his thumb and unrolled it until he had a fairly generous amount in his hand.

"That's more than enough," Lexi said,

reaching for the bundle in his hand "Here, cut it right between my fingers."

"With wha—?" He noticed Sarah gesturing for him to grab her brother's pocket knife, then tossing it right at him. He caught it—hoping to any deity that listened that the blade wouldn't open as he did so—and inspected it briefly. The soft, exquisitely carved wooden handle felt smooth all along the edges, its brown stain shining in the morning light, and in the small cracks of usage, Alex saw the silver blade peeking through at him. He flicked the blade, nervously avoiding the edge, and slid it between where Lexi's fingers were, cutting through like air itself. He closed the blade and tossed it back to Sarah.

"About damned time. Roll the rest up and stick it back in the box."

Lexi turned to begin wrapping Sarah's bloody hand. First, she stuck the piece of gauze under Sarah's thumb, then began wrapping the wound. Sarah's continued twirling of the knife in her hand was distracting, but Lexi continued wrapping.

As the knife twirled between Sarah's fingers and around her palm, she found her eyes slowly drawing back to the sharp, beaten handle which had cut her so deeply. She didn't consider herself superstitious by any means, but after the events of the past two days, she wasn't exactly sure what to believe.

"All right, done," Lexi said, placing the small bit of tape over the lip of gauze. "Now, how about we take the next few steps a bit more carefully." She winked, but there was a hint of fear in her eyes.

"You got it, Kitty," Alex said. "How about we start with using this box? You got some useful stuff in here."

"Grab whatever you think we'll need. My mom can get it refilled if necessary," she said, waving back at him as she joined Sam and Tammy, who were staring through the blackness of the open door.

Sarah stood beside him, deciding what to take along with them. She pointed towards the Band-Aids, but Alex shook his head. "Too small. If anything we should bring the gauze," he whispered to himself. Sarah grabbed the flashlight, a few Band-Aids, and the bottle of disinfectant, and stuffed them in the pockets of her black jeans. She took one last look at the box, deciding nothing else was of much use, and turned to walk away.

Alex stared blankly into the box, his eyes darting between the flare-torch and the jumbo sized gauze wrap. Among them were smaller tools that *might* prove useful; some tweezers, a small pair of scissors, and a few pills of ibuprofen. He grabbed the handful of ibuprofen and the long wrap of gauze, and stuffed them into his pockets. He turned to leave, but turned back towards the torch.

"I can't see anything," Tammy said, staring through the now opened iron door.

"Yeah," Samuel added. "Maybe there's

a light switch or something?" He stepped through the doorway.

"What the hell, K9?!" Tammy screeched behind him, making him jump in surprise.

"What?" He shrugged. "You don't believe in ghosts, do you, Tammy?"

"N...no...." Tammy backed away, clenching tight on her small backpack, inside of which was her whole life; her tablet.

"Then there's nothing to be afraid of," Sam said, gesturing for the others to follow.

Sarah turned back, expecting Alex to be right behind her. He was a few feet away, grabbing at his pocket in a sort of worried fear, but it quickly subsided as he pulled the small silver lighter out, breathing a sigh of relief. By the time he was by her side, she had already flicked the flashlight and illuminated the shadowy innards of the game-and-stop, surprising the others with the sudden shine of light.

"Woah...," Lexi whispered.

The walls were lined with all the signs

of decay; the moldy green splotches up and down each surface along the corridor, the cracked and broken down walls, the disgustingly discolored patterns along the floor — which all seemed to be marked with some sort of dry sludge from which the kids were more than keen on keeping their distance — and the mortifying odor of an age of horror. It took a moment, but as their eyes acclimated to the thick air and dark corridor, they began to notice the streak of red along the right side of the floor, right beside the wall that led through the corridor into the employee's only area. On the ground was a long "Happy Birthday Ricky!" banner with a faded bloody handprint on the side.

The group had to cover their mouths and noses, trying desperately to keep the horrid stench from attacking their senses, but to no avail. They coughed and heaved for a few moments before any of them could catch their breaths. Sarah felt her eyes water, Alex gripped at his chest, and Samuel tried his best to keep from vomiting up his breakfast.

"Everyone...all right?" Alex said at last, after more than enough painful hacking and choking on the putrid, thick air.

Everyone nodded one by one, leaving Tammy the last to raise a thumb in agreement, despite still heaving heavily. Sam kneeled beside her, patting her back and hoping for the best.

"It's terrible in here." His cough returned while he spoke. "Do you guys really think this is a good idea?"

"We need to at least try to look," Alex responded, starting forward, his cough seeming to subside. "We promised Sarah we'd help find him, and this is the first step."

"Well, Hoot's clearly not handling it all that well. Maybe we should come back with gas masks or something."

"Where in this town do you expect to buy a gas mask, let alone five of them?" Responded Sarah, moving to stand beside Alex. "I'm not forcing any of you to stay here with me, but I need to check, just to be sure."

"I'm fine," Tammy stated, rising to her feet. "Don't worry about me, I won't be any burden."

"Are you sure, Hoot?" Samuel asked, his hand was still firmly planted on her shoulder.

"Lay off, K9." She shoved him back. "I can handle myself."

"Fine, fine." Samuel raised his hands in mock defense. "But let's set a rule: If you're having trouble breathing—or any trouble really—speak up. The last thing we need is for someone to cut their leg open and not say anything. Deal?"

They all nodded in agreement, last of which was Alex, solemnly raising a thumb to the others behind him before starting down the hall, followed closely by the rest of the group. Sarah quickly made her way to Alex's side, curious of why he was so intent on something so dangerous.

"So…," she said, unsure where to begin.

"This place looks like a horror show," he muttered in response.

"Yeah, like some kind of ghost or monster would jump out from the walls at any moment."

"And it's huge. Maybe we should split up for a bit. You know, to cover more ground."

"Did you guys say split up?!" Cried Lexi from the back. "Have you guys, like, *never* seen horror movies before? That's where it starts!"

"Dibs on not having Kit in my group," muttered Sam, which brought a chuckle from Tammy, still at his side.

"I heard that, Pooch!" Screeched Lexi. "I'm just saying that maybe splitting isn't a good idea!"

"This isn't a movie, Kit," Sarah responded in a calm tone. "There isn't a ghost around here that will come out and possess you, I promise."

"Or a monster to eat you," added Tammy.

"All right. But I want Snake in my group."

"Hey, that's not fair!" Said Tammy. "She should choose the groups! Her and Leo!"

"Fine." Sarah turned to Alex. "What do you think?"

"Girls one side, guys the other?" He responded, still staring straight down the dank, disgusting corridor. "You girls take the flashlight. I've got pretty good eyesight and some other things to help us down here." He winked at her.

"All right then." She looked nervously at him. "Hoot, Kit, and I will go through the arcade."

"K9 and I will take the game stands and shops. Bound to be something there," Alex added.

"Well, good luck everybody!" Sarah exclaimed.

Sarah led her group through the large

door with the neon sign above which had once read FIRELIGHT ARCADE. She stared up at the dead sign curiously. In the years before the place was shut down, the firelight arcade was one of the biggest hangouts for kids and adults who loved video games. It brought back the memories of her brother playing his dumb shooter or racing games. He'd let her have a turn, of course, but she was never any good at it. She wondered if any of those games would still be there. She pushed open the rusty old door.

***

"You think they'll still have some old cartridge games here?" Asked Samuel as the two passed through the door labeled BUY & SELL. "I hear old games can sell for a ton of cash."

"Stay focused, K9," said Alex, not unkindly. "We're looking for Erik, remember?"

"Of course Erik is top priority, but I mean if we could make a few bucks while we're at it...."

"Ugh...." Alex sighed, waving him off to look at the shelves.

Samuel approached the supposedly empty shelves along the wall and scrounged around. Laying on the ground were several opened game boxes, some of which he even recognized; some old *Sonic the Hedgehog* games were on the floor, a few *Earthbound* cases were lying under the shelves, and there were even cases for a few different *Mario* games.

Samuel fiddled through the boxes, finding nothing but dust and a few tiny white spiders hanging around inside one of them. He laid the box down on its side and let the little spiders free. They crawled away for a moment before slipping down through a crack in the floor and disappearing.

Alex fiddled with the handle, but the door wouldn't push open. He ran his finger along the DO NOT ENTER sign below the office title. He pulled his fingers back and wiped the dust off them before grabbing the handle once again. Twisting with all his might, the handle finally gave way to his force, cranking open the small gears in the latch and pushing the door open, if only an inch.

Alex peeked through the gap, but the shadowy office was too dark to see through. He took a step back then rushed forward with all his force, smashing his shoulder against the door. It swung open with a loud CRASH, shaking the walls and surprising Samuel.

"What the hell was that?" Asked Samuel from the other end of the room.

"Just me. Door wouldn't open, but I got it," Alex responded, grabbing his lighter from his pocket. He flicked the wheel until the flame sparked to life. With what little illumination the flame provided, he inspected the strange office. Along the milky, off-white wall, lined with water stains and patches of what looked like dark green mold, were a few small filing cabinets. In the corner was a computer desk, with what used to be a monitor sitting atop, and an empty slot where the computer itself once sat.

"Well at least they got the computer out," Alex thought, only to find he had spoken aloud.

Along the other wall was a larger desk—clearly meant for the owner of this establishment, while the smaller was meant for an assistant of some kind. Atop the desk was a pair of small monitors, each attached to the desk at opposing corners, which both faced the decrepit and ripped apart chair on which the owner must've sat. Alex approached the desk, taking note of the waste of fine craftsmanship, and the countless scratches and broken pieces. The desk looked clearly ready to fall apart.

Alex delicately opened the drawer, jumping back as a pair of small spiders crawled through the opening, barely missing his hands as they jumped out to the floor.

They crawled through his legs until they reached a crack in the floor beneath the leg of the desk and disappeared. He stared at the hole for a moment, attempting to move the table's leg to get a better look, but as the wood split and cracked in his hands, he thought better of it.

Alex fiddled through the drawer; there was a few small dusty pencils, a large box that, when opened, showed there was nothing inside, and a bundle of paper, carpeted with dust. He pulled the bundle out of the drawer, shutting it quickly as to avoid another encounter with the spiders.

Beneath the bundle of paper was a small brown envelope. On the front was the name Doctor LeCrane, and the back was sealed with black wax and pressed in the shape of a large D. Alex reached in and grabbed the envelope and shoved it into his back pocket before throwing the first bundle onto the desk, sending dust and scraps of wood flying in the resulting breath of wind.

"Crypto-Aranea…." Alex mouthed the title at the top of the page.

***

"Woah! It's *Blasterzz*!" Lexi said skipping towards the small boxed arcade game.

"Well it's not like it's gonna work, Kit," Tammy said, adjusting her glasses. "Do you know how long this place has been closed down?"

"I can still pretend. I loved this game!" Lexi grabbed at the plastic model of what she called the Blaster — which looked more like a child's idea of what an alien gun might look like — and aimed it at the other two girls. "All right, humans." She tried her best alien voice, though it turned out to be almost exactly the same as her normal voice. "Time to beg for mercy from Quag-zar the beautiful."

"Quag-zar?" Whispered Tammy.

"It's her pretend name. Remember when we used to play aliens at my old house?" Sarah responded with a slight chuckle.

"Be silent, humans!" Lexi stated. "Hold your tongues unless your next words are for mercy."

"Please, Quag-zar!" Cried Sarah, "I have no means of escape, yet I have so much to live for! Please spare my life, and I will be yours forever more!" She bowed her head as close to the ground as she could, without actually touching the small green sludge pile inches away from her face.

"And what of you, small one?" Lexi pointed the gun at Tammy.

"I will not be begging for mercy today, alien!" Tammy grabbed the flashlight out of Sarah's hand and shone it upon Lexi's face. "For I have the power of light on my side! Feel the stinging pain of the sun, beast!" She tried her best to make her voice sound threatening, though her childlike tone always seeped through.

"Aaagggghhh!" Lexi screeched, grasping at her chest. The smile made its way to her face, and soon after a melody of laughter broke out from the three of them. It wasn't long before they were all hung over laughing. Sarah wondered as the laughter left her body why they were all laughing at all.

Is it really that funny? Or is it just our need to lighten the mood that makes us joke and laugh in the darkest moments? She thought, but refused to say it out loud. "All right guys, enough playing." Sarah's laughter finally subsided. "Let's look around. Don't leave any stone unturned!" She raised her fist in a triumphant pose, but dropped it after receiving curious looks from the other two.

She turned and made her way towards the back of the arcade. The machines along the way interested her, several of them being familiar. *Armored Raceway* and *Battle of the Brutes* were the two she remembered most fondly playing alongside her brother whenever he took her to the arcade as a young girl.

She fiddled with the small joystick on

Battle of the Brutes, reminiscing about all the times her brother had crushed her at the game. Her small smile slowly faded away as her fingers touched the joystick her brother had used, feeling the ridges of the handle and the strange stickiness of the buttons. She hesitantly let go and moved on.

Lexi trotted over to a small racing game, which had once used a moving chair to simulate the car, and had a strikingly accurate representation of a steering wheel. When it came to *Firelight Arcade*, the crazier everything looked, the better. Yet this car was set to be so realistic that whenever Lexi had played as a kid, she felt like she was really at the race course.

She sat down in the hard rough metal chair—checking for creepy crawlies all through the cracks and corners—and placed her back against the seat. The memories suddenly flew back to her as she reached for the steering wheel. The leather wrap was old and worn and reeked of age, but it felt oddly comfortable in her hand. She could see herself in the race. Not in the game, no, but in a real race car, racing alongside twenty — no, fifty — other racers for the grand prize of a million dollars. In her mind's eye she saw the light count down. Three. Two. One.

Tammy wasn't nearly as interested in the random assortment of arcade games as the other two. She took a seat by the entrance, opening her tablet to continue reading her book. The bright light stunned her for a moment, but eventually her eyes acclimated to the new bright screen. She opened her online reading program and started the new book entitled *Hellsing Hospital.*

Barely a few pages into the story, she noticed something out the corner of her eye; a fat white blob that crawled along the wall to her right. The spider closed in on her, barely a few inches away from her face before stopping to stare at the girl. Tammy stared back, unafraid. Spiders had never frightened her too much. She'd read about thousands of different spider types, and none of them lived anywhere near her. But this one was a curious find. She threw out her hand for the spider. It cautiously climbed onto her hand and stopped in her palm.

Tammy inspected the spider; it was abnormally large, yes, but its white skin was what truly made her curious. Of all the spider varieties in Witchern, or anywhere around, there hadn't been any pure white varieties until very recently. She took a closer look, inching her hand closer and closer to her eyes, but stopped suddenly. She saw something in the reflection of her large glasses. Something was behind her, something white.

***

"Hey K9!" Alex said from the office, ruffling through the filing cabinets for more information. "Come here a minute!"

"What's up, Leo?" He asked, entering the room, which was significantly more destroyed than it had been when Alex entered. "Dude, what happened in here?!"

"What do you mean? I'm just looking around. Here, help me look through these files."

"For what? We're supposed to be looking for Erik. You think he's hiding in a file cabinet?"

"No, but—"

"Dude, I can't find anything out here. Let's move on—maybe the girls found something."

"You go on ahead—I'll be right there. If the girls haven't found anything just start on the other buildings without me. I'll be out shortly."

"What the hell are you looking for in here?"

"Go!" Alex snapped. "I mean, the girls might have found something—go find out."

"Whatever you say, Leo."

Samuel's shut down tone and glazed face made Alex want to pull him back to apologize, but he was too busy. "They'll be fine for a moment," whispered Alex. "I need to find more information."

He lined the papers along the old wooden desk. Many of the pages were faded to nothing, and what little he could read was small portions of a bigger, more important part of the situation that was recaptured in these pages.

"Crypto-Aranea. Neurotoxic venom… presents itself when feeding…loud 'hissing' sound…bursts from host's body…." Alex tried to make use of what little information he could, but none of it made any sense to him until he reached the final literate portion of the last page. "Venom is extremely flammable. Make all necessary precautions to assure the cryptid remains below."

"Flammable venom?" He flicked his lighter again, noticing the small pile of green sludge on the ground beside the table. He grinned slightly.

***

"C'mon get outta my way, jackass!" Lexi said, still sitting in the broken metal race car chair.

Second place now, in her mind's eye she was nearing the finish line. The last racer swerved in front of her car. She pulled left and right trying to get herself around the heaping black car. The last turn was approaching, and she could see the finish line. With one final drifting turn, pulling back as hard as possible on the steering wheel, she managed to skid past the side of the black car and take the lead, bursting across the finish line in a beautiful photo-finish. She burst up from the chair with a cry of pride, only to return to the dank dark arcade she had once been in.

"Everything all right, Kit?" Asked Samuel, entering the arcade behind her.

"Jeez, K9, scared the hell outta me!" She said, grasping at her chest. "What are you doing here? I thought you and Leo were checking out the game shops."

"Nothing out of the ordinary there—a few old game boxes and a few spiders, but nothing useful. Alex is scrounging around an old office looking through papers, told us to go on looking without him for a while. Where're the other girls?"

"I'm right here," Sarah said, popping up from behind him. He jumped away, hiding behind the much smaller Lexi with a mild yelp.

"God, Snake, don't do that," he said, brushing himself down, trying to maintain his cool-guy look.

"Sorry, K9, guess every dog has his day."

"Watch it." He prodded his finger into her arm. "A dog could easily eat a snake, right Hoot?"

There was no response.

"Hoot? Where's Tammy?" Asked Samuel.

"Kit, wasn't she right next to you?" Asked Sarah.

"I thought she went with you," she

responded.

"Guys, it doesn't matter who she was with, we have to find her. You two start looking around here. I'll grab Alex and meet you in the back — in that employee only area back there."

"Okay, let's go Kit." Sarah grabbed her by the wrist and dragged her out the door.

***

"Come on, dammit!" Alex kicked at it again, and finally the jointed leg smashed off the table, landing beside the other three laying out on the ground. He dropped the table on the ground and stuffed the papers in his back pocket. The table legs were roughly round enough to fit in the palm of his hand, though they grew and extended as they reached the point where the table would sit upon them. Alex pulled the gauze wrap and began wrapping a generous amount around the widest point of the leg, and then did the same for the other three. He set those three aside and approached the small pile of green sludge with the first leg, dipped the gauze-wrapped head in, then swirled it around to coat the entire tip. The smell was so foul it burned his nostrils and ripped at his insides.

"What the actual hell are you doing?!" Shouted Samuel from the doorway.

"Jesus, man." Alex nearly dropped the leg in surprise. "Hey, watch this." He flicked the wheel of his lighter, igniting the flame, and ran it along the damp green gauze. Instantly it burst aflame, lighting the entire room like a flashlight. "Maybe now we can see a bit better. Sarah can keep the flashlight. Here, grab these three, there's one for each of us."

"Tammy's gone."

Alex's excited grin quickly faded to a horrified look. He shut his lighter and stormed out, gesturing for Samuel to grab the rest of the torches.

***

Tammy's eyes finally focused, as best they could without her glasses — which were

117

laying at the other end of the rocky cave. She tried to move, but found her arms and legs unresponsive. She looked down at the white wrapping all around her body. The thick, scratchy threads dug into her arms. The more she moved the more she felt it sawing into her flesh.

She sat as still as possible trying and hoping to think of some way to help. Her vision was blurry, but she could make out the shapes of stalactites and gashes in the stone walls, along with the hundred moving white specks all along the floor, moving towards the wide opening at the other end. They were moving away from some reddish shape at her side she couldn't make out. She sat silently watching the spiders skitter their way out of the cave, until the last one turned the corner out of sight.

Tammy dropped to her side, crashing against a group of sharp rocks that stabbed into her sides. With the few movement possibilities at her disposal, she eventually slithered her way over to her glasses, maneuvering them onto her face as best she could without the use of her hands. The cracks and scratches made seeing difficult, but her vision was much better now that she had the glasses on. She tried to prop herself up on the rocky wall, but flopped back down on her side, staring straight at that red shape from which all those spiders had come. Her heart dropped instantly, and an inaudible gasp came up as she stared blankly at the wide gaping hole in the man's torso. Calling it a torso would be too generous, as it was ripped to shreds from the inside. She felt the tears run down her cheeks, and it took everything she had not to scream when she saw the small silver half-heart pendant hanging loosely in the gaping hole where Erik's chest would've been.

***

Erik limped as fast as possible. His groggy bones and blurry vision made it nearly impossible to see where he was going in the dark tunnel. Nevertheless, he continued forward, balancing himself on the rough, spiky, stone wall, shredding his hands as they dragged him along. His stump leg crashed painfully against the ground. Searing pain ran through both of his legs, like a hot iron pressed firmly against each and every inch of flesh he had. He wondered if his bones were as close to breaking as they felt.

SNAP. They were.

His stumped leg skidded along a large spire and twisted against the ground. He felt the bone break under his weight as he fell. He could see just ahead of him the darkness of the arcade, the beautifully decrepit exit from this hell in which he found himself. He pulled himself along with his arms, slicing scrapes and scars all along his body. He felt he would make it, like he could finally escape, until the sudden clawing began to climb up his leg towards him.

Instinctively he looked over his shoulder.

The hundreds of small spiders were making their way up both of his legs, while the larger ones were crawling around him. Above him, on the ceiling of the tunnel, he saw the fully grown spiders—easily six feet long, front to back, and three feet high on all eight legs. They started descending towards him, the enormous, thick threads of silk protruding from their abdomens. He watched the bright red eyes come closer and closer to him. He closed his eyes and planted his face to the ground to wait for the inevitable.

Suddenly there was a crack, and a bright light appeared in front of him. The spiders all scampered back, fleeing from the flaming light coming from the tunnel opening. The giant spiders climbed their way back to the ceiling, then slowly backed away from the bright flare and the man holding it.

"Stand up, son." The man's voice was deep and coarse, but not unkind.

Erik felt the last few spiders crawling away from him, and pushed himself up onto his good foot, balancing himself on the wall beside him. He limped his way towards the man holding the bright red flare, nearly falling over in front of him. The man barely caught him in his free arm. He seemed an old man, grey in the hair and a full white beard on his pale face. In his old age, he didn't seem quite strong enough to hold up Erik's admittedly heavy body, but he seemed to be doing it with relative ease. He held the torch above Erik's face, taking a good look at the boy. It was only now that Erik felt the countless scars across his face, and the hundred different stabbing pains in his body.

The man propped Erik up against the wall. With his now free hand, he reached in and gripped the small pendant between his fingers.

"A nice trinket...." He felt the fine craftsmanship of the silver, then let it fall back at his chest. "But I think I'd prefer these," he said, reaching into Erik's pockets, pulling out the star shaped key ring and fiddling with it in his fingers.

"Wait...I need help." Erik's voice was fading again. "Please...."

"Oh I'm sorry, son," the man said. "I'm only here to clean up a mess. And the way I see it, you're already dead." He gestured towards Erik's stomach.

Erik felt beneath his shirt. The small scar was pulsating, and he could feel the intense pain growing ever more painful second by second. He wanted to scream, but all that would come out was, "Please...."

"Goodnight, my boy," the man said, before making his way back towards the entrance of the arcade.

The light began to fade as the man left through the arcade. And as the door shut behind him, the light faded to nothing but a small glow beneath the space under the door. Erik felt the spiny footsteps closing in on him again, growing and clawing at his flesh. He didn't fight it any longer — he knew he couldn't possibly win that fight. So he let go, and allowed them to drag his limp body back to wherever they wished. The last thing he heard before his consciousness passed was the hissing. That horrid hissing....

THE SPIDER

"Hoot!" Lexi called into the giant tunnel.

Sarah stood beside her, shining the flashlight around, watching it bounce off each small shining stone. She turned at the sound of the door opening to the arcade. Alex and Samuel burst through holding the wooden torches, only Alex's was lit.

"What are those?" Asked Sarah.

Lexi turned to see. "A bit old-school, isn't it?" Asked Lexi.

"Look," Alex said, waving the torch with emphasis. "I've got a bit of a hunch as to what's going on here, but I can't really

125

explain it right now. Just everyone take a torch. I'll light it, and if you see any spiders, no matter what size, wave them away with the fire. Under no circumstances do you let them get near you, is that understood?"

"What the hell are you talking about?" demanded Sarah, taking the unlit torch from Samuel.

"Just trust me on this! If Tammy's gone missing, we might not have a lot of time left." He flicked his lighter and lit the other three torches. "We all stay together now — no one leaves the pack unattended."

"Like I said from the start!" Lexi shouted.

"Yes, Lexi, you were right — want a medal? We don't have time for this! Let's go find her."

As the other three started down the tunnel, Lexi stopped, noticing the large bloodstain set in the tiled floor that led down into the tunnel, like someone had dragged a sack of red paint all across the floor and thrown it against the opening. Lexi slowly followed behind the others, tracing her eyes along the long trail of blood on the ground, which gradually thinned to a small splotch here and there along the ground and wall.

She inspected a splotch of blood on the wall: it was almost in the shape of a handprint, like someone was propping them-self against the wall as they ascended the tunnel. She wondered briefly if it was Erik's—

"Lex, come on!" Sarah shouted from the bottom of the tunnel, waving her torch at her.

"Coming!" She hurried to their side. "Guys, there's a lot of blood along the walls here."

The three closed in, examining the blood. Sarah pulled the pocketknife from her side pocket, twirling it between her fingers. She flicked the blade open and pressed the tip lightly against the splotch of blood on the wall. The small trickle of red that slowly made its way down the silver blade confirmed it to the three.

"It's recent," muttered Samuel. "You think it's—?"

Sarah clicked the blade shut before anyone could answer, shoving the wooden handle back into her pocket. She was the first to turn, followed shortly by the two boys. Lexi had difficulty in taking her eyes away from the deep red handprint of blood splattered against the spire. She watched the reflection of the flickering torch in the bright red print.

"Hey!" Said Samuel, tapping the back of her shoulder, pulling her from the red vision. "Come on. No one gets lost."

"Oh, right—coming." The two of them took their places at the sides of the others.

They stood at a split tunnel. Both led into complete darkness, and what sounded like small rocks trickling through the walls.

"All right, which way?" Asked Sarah, to no one in particular.

"Each way seems the same," muttered

Alex. "See, this is the place we'd normally split up. Perhaps we should take that tunnel." He pointed down the right tunnel.

"Why that one?" Asked Samuel.

"Because it's the one we're all staring at, and it's the one making the hissing sound."

It took the other three a moment to hear it, but the strange whisper of a hiss slowly rose from nothing, until it was nearly all they could hear. And it was, indeed, coming from the right tunnel.

"No such thing as monsters, eh K9?" Jested Lexi, though the shivers up and down her spine were less than a joke.

"Hold on a sec. Why would we go *towards* the terrifying hissing?"

"Gotta play the odds, K9," suggested Alex. "You've seen those old monster movies, right? The monster always takes the girl back to its lair. So we find the monster...."

"We find Hoot," added Lexi.

"And my brother...," finished Sarah,

pressing her fingers against the golden heart around her neck.

***

Tammy watched in abject horror as the giant spiders slowly passed the large open entrance to the cave, occasionally stopping to stare in her direction. The strange way their eyes all moved in synchronicity to dart towards her in an instant wasn't something she'd thought possible when she saw their smaller cousins in her mother's attic. She felt the urge to scream crawling up her throat with every passing second, seeing the smaller—yet still abnormally large— hairy bodies crawling unnaturally around the cave walls. The tingling sensation that thrust its way through her motionless nerves as their tiny, sharpened legs jabbed holes in her flesh as they crawled over her body made her want to shake and squirm like a wet dog.

Her eyes kept swapping between the large open cave entrance, surrounded by white death, and the man who once was called Erik, her best friend's older brother. She couldn't imagine the horrific way in which he must've died, though she didn't spend much time thinking on that, in truth.

She gritted her teeth, the sudden surge of pain coming from inside her stomach showing itself again, much worse than before. Her stomach felt like it was bloating, or exploding altogether. Sweat dripped down her face, matting her hair to her head and forcing her glasses to slide down her nose and crack against one of the spiders sitting quietly on her lap. The spider hissed and climbed up to take a seat on the top of her head. The shivers made her feel like she was having some sort of minor seizure.

Suddenly the strange hissing started again, growing closer and closer. She could feel the quaking steps of that horrid, giant monster making its way to her cave, until finally she saw it.

The enormous white spider poked

its head through the cave entrance. The chelicerae were drenched with thick, green venom, which dripped down into a puddle on the ground beneath it. Its face alone was nearly enormous enough to completely fill the hole of a doorway, but it pressed through. One leg appeared — a thick, spiny leg — and stabbed viciously into the ground, penetrating the hard rock floor over a foot deep, showing just where all the uneven holes were coming from. A second leg crashed into the ground, then a third. It slowly pushed its giant body in through the cave, knocking spires and stalactites off the walls and ceiling. They crashed to the ground with an explosion. The spider's final two legs bent unnaturally through the door, pulling the large, web filled abdomen through like a bulbous sack of mucus. The eyes stared down at the girl, slowly bending its head towards her, close enough that she could feel the hairs on the chelicera rubbing against her face.

She closed her eyes, waiting for whatever mortifying fate awaited her. There was a sound, like a wet fruit opening up, or perhaps being crushed under intense force. She felt the hairs tingle off her face, and opened her eyes.

The spiders face was inches away from the body of her old friend, motionlessly staring at him. On top of the spider's head was the torso, arms, and head of a thin woman. Her flowing white hair draped down her back like a waterfall. Her eyes were red, and numerous—four in total, two in each place where Tammy herself had one. Her pale, thin arms were thrusting forward at Erik's once lively face, clawing at him with the black, long, knife-like claws at the ends of her fingertips.

Tammy stared awestruck at the woman. Were she not coming out from a hideously enormous spider, she would've been beautiful, if a bit pale. The small white flaps of spider skin hung open at her hips.

The woman seemed to be…eating Erik's face. Her black claws left barbaric gashes in his flesh, and pulled chunks towards her razor sharp teeth. Tammy watched in horror as the last bits of Erik's face were slowly ripped from him and stuffed into the mouth of this terrifying creature. The small silver pendant flew across the cave as she swiped, crashing against a spire in the corner of the cave and bouncing to the ground.

***

"Tammy!" Sarah shouted down the empty, inky-black tunnel.

The waving flames of the torches flickered shadows on the wall, dancing along with them as they walked. It was almost mesmerizing in a way, the unnatural way they moved and passed over depressions and raised stones along the wall seamlessly. Samuel stopped briefly to feel the indentations of the wall. They felt like crushed stone on the inside, like a giant metal pole was stuffed forcefully through the surface of the rock, and pulled out just as forcefully.

There was a sound, rising slowly from the darkness behind them. A skittering rush of tapping, like a hailstorm on a glass roof, resounding off the walls behind him.

Samuel quickly brushed his torch behind him, waving it back and forth at all the tiny red eyes that quickly appeared from the shadows. Sweat dripped down his brow as he twirled the torch around like a flaming tornado.

"Guys!" He screamed.

The three of them turned back to see the army of tiny spiders bursting towards them. Kit was the first to arrive at his side, shaking the torch along the walls. The larger, more terrifying spiders were beginning to make their way along the ceiling, cracking their fangs together with menacing clacks. Samuel raised his torch to the giant spiders, while Alex stepped in front of him and waved his own at the lower level, catching the spiders in the face. Sarah stood at his side, slashing at the spiders with her torch. They watched the flaming spiders rush back into the crowd, hiding in the sea of white.

A small patch caught Alex's eye, a green puddle of slime that was still sticky, judging by the spiders slight struggle to pass over it. He rushed towards it, swinging his torch around his legs before finally stabbing it into the green puddle setting it ablaze. The burst of fire sent the spiders skittering back down the tunnel in fear. Alex felt the explosion of fire sending him back more than a few feet into the wall of the tunnel, cracking the back of his head against a flat stone. His vision blurred, but refocused quickly. He saw the spiders fleeing, and their moment to escape.

"Run!" Alex shouted, instinctively grabbing Sarah's hand and dragging her along at his side.

They frantically rushed through the sharp, rocky tunnel, waving their torches behind in circles at their feet as, behind them, the thousand beady red eyes pursued. The shadowy tunnel was a tornado of red eyes spiraling as far as the tunnel went.

The hissing grew louder in front of them as they went. They began to feel it shaking their eardrums. Alex gripped tightly on his torch, whitening his already pale knuckles.

Sarah felt something slimy beneath her foot with each step. She looked down to see a trail of slimy green sludge. She gestured to Alex, gripping tightly on his hand and pointing her torch towards it. He nodded, a slight smile creeping across his face.

"Light it," he said.

She dragged the tip of her torch along the line of green slime. It burst into an explosion of fire, running down the tunnel in both directions, lighting their way. The spiders behind them began to shriek and cry. The fire illuminated their horrific faces, and lit a clear line of them on fire. They scampered around unnaturally, crashing into each other, spreading the fire amongst each of them until they scattered back down the tunnel in fear. The flickering flames of the burning spiders danced around the tunnel and grew, and spread. The group wondered how many had just burned, or if they had ignited any other venom piles on their way. They knew the answer when another sudden explosion of fire burst from the end of the tunnel.

The hissing sound grew to a screech, crashing against their ear drums like the sound of a hundred shotgun shells. Lexi dropped her torch, gripping the sides of her head and squeezing tightly. Samuel did the same, crouching at her side. Sarah managed to keep hold of her torch with one hand, pressing the other against her temple. Alex, meanwhile, seemed least affected by the sudden hissing burst, lightly pressing his hand against his forehead as he stared down the line of dancing flames.

Soon enough, the hissing slowly subsided. Sarah opened her tightly shut eyes to see the flaming trail she had left. Alex stared curiously at it before gesturing for the others to follow. Samuel and Lexi picked up their torches, reignited them in the new flames, and followed behind them.

The burning trail led to a small puddle of what was once the thick, green venom, burning like a bonfire. The flame slowly drooped and faded until it all but disappeared into the shadow. Sarah was the first to walk into the giant cave, illuminating the horrid, mortifying cavern. The smell was terrible, but the scene of half mutilated bodies and hundreds of skeletal remains lying all over the ground was much, much worse. Along the walls were even more bodies, with their chests and stomachs burst from their insides, like a grenade had exploded inside of them.

Alex and Samuel walked around the other side of the cave. Samuel couldn't take his eyes off the dreadful sight of the bodies leaning against the walls. Some even seemed to be stuck higher on the wall, with some sort of thick white wrapping. He couldn't make out what it was, but in his heart he already knew.

Alex made his way towards the back of the cave, spotting some small sheen on the ground in the corner. He knelt down, balancing himself on the small stalagmite, and picked up the small silver pendant, wiping the dirt and blood off it. The small half-heart pendant shone beautifully in the torchlight.

"Erik," he muttered to himself, feeling his heart drop into his stomach.

"What did you find, Leo?" Asked Samuel, still lamenting over the decaying corpses.

"Sarah, you might want to see this," Alex said, slowly approaching her. He held out his hand and showed her the small heart.

She reached for it, stopping briefly with a heavy breath. Tears covered her eyes until she felt like a waterfall was about to come raging down her cheeks. She palmed the pendant, feeling the soft silver beneath her thumb. She felt Lexi's arm wrap around her shoulder, and Samuel's soft pats on her other.

"Wh…where did you find it?" She said, wiping her eyes.

Alex pointed to the back corner where he'd found the heart.

"There wasn't a—" She stopped suddenly, catching a small white blob in the shadows of the cave. "Wait, what is that?"

The four of them approached the small white bundle laying up against the back wall of the cave. It remained motionless, and as they neared it, the shape slowly came into focus.

"Tammy!" Lexi shouted, rushing towards the small bundle of webbing with the tiny head poking out the top. "Tammy! Tammy!" She shook Tammy's head back and forth, giving it a quick slap. "Wake up, kid! Your mom's gonna kill me if I don't get you home!"

Sarah ran to her side, but stopped suddenly, noticing the exploded body sitting beside Tammy. The face was mangled to hell, and the torso was virtually eviscerated. Still, there was something in the broken and beaten bones along the body that brought her unyielding grief. She didn't need to confirm it — she knew who it was.

Tammy was silent. None of them could tell if she was alive. The webbing gave no signs of breathing, and her pale, thin face looked like that of a skeleton. Sarah dropped her torch to the ground and pulled the knife from her pocket, flicking the blade out. She slowly prodded it through the silky webbing, slicing a thin opening down the front of the round bundle, then dropped the knife to the ground and ripped the rest of the wrapping off by hand, pulling and tearing at the web until there was a wide enough opening. Samuel threw his torch aside and reached in to grab one shoulder while she reached in for the other. With all their strength they pulled and pulled until they finally felt the ripping sound and pulled her out, tumbling back onto the ground.

"Tammy, wake the hell up!" Sarah cried, shaking the young girl's shoulders back and forth.

"I thought you said there was no such things as monsters," Tammy whispered, opening her eyes a crack.

"Tell us about it when we get out of here," said Alex. "I'm sure Mama will be back soon enough."

"Mama?" Sarah asked. "What do you mean, 'Mama'?"

"What, you think all these giant-ass spiders just appeared from nowhere?"

"He's right...," Tammy's voice was weak, coming out as only a hushed whisper. "Mama will be back soon, you need to leave."

"*We* need to leave," corrected Samuel. "We're not leaving you behind."

"You don't understand. I'm already...."

143

She gestured to the wound in her stomach. "They'll come soon, you need to run."

"I don't understand, what the hell are you talking about?"

"She's a host," whispered Alex, suddenly realizing the situation. "It was in the notes in the office. She's right, we need to leave, now." Alex started towards the exit.

"We can't leave her here!" Shouted Sarah. "We came all this way for them, and now we're leaving her in this hell hole?!"

"Sarah, you don't—"

Tammy's sudden screech of pain pulled everyone's eyes. She shook and jerked violently in Sarah's arms, pushing her away and falling to the ground with a crash. Her arms flailed about, grasping futilely at the air before wrapping tightly around her stomach. Her deafening scream resounded in the walls, like the wail of a dying baby. Sarah backed away. All they could do was watch as the small girl flailed painfully on the ground, jerking back and forth with her terrible cries of pain.

Suddenly she stopped, her glassy gaze staring up at nothing. There was the trembling sound of bones breaking, and a sound which could only be described as that of bursting innards. Tammy's stomach suddenly started pulsating, and moving beneath the skin. There was a sound of quiet hissing, and then her shirt slowly faded to a red stain. Her stomach seemed to expand endlessly, turning the unnaturally small, young girl into a distended ball, with thousands of moving parts inside.

There was a sudden popping sound, and the four of them watched in abject horror as Tammy's stomach burst in a bloody explosion, sending thousands of small white spiders flying through the air at them. Sarah pulled back quickly, barely avoiding the raining spiders. Samuel stayed for a moment, stunned in awe of what was happening before his eyes. He felt the sudden jerk of the back of his collar and flew back to the ground, narrowly avoiding the clenching fangs of thousands of hungry spiderlings. He looked up at Alex's horror-struck look, and stood to run alongside them.

***

They sprinted down the tunnel, following the black, charred stones on the ground as their guiding path. Alex led the group, waving his torch at any creature that would come, big or small. At the back, Sarah had taken hold of the other remaining torch, waving off the fresh new wave of newborn spiders crawling towards them at a surprisingly swift speed. She waved the torch, catching any that tried prematurely jumping at her legs. Their screeching, flaming bodies tumbled back through the wave, lighting several other spiders along the way, yet not nearly enough to show a dent in the thousands still chasing her.

They ducked and weaved through the tunnels, following the charred path back to the arcade, and to freedom. Alex pounded his torch into another puddle of slime, exploding it into a fiery burst, sending the spiders ahead of them running in fear.

"This way!" He shouted, climbing the giant tunnel.

The others followed suit, climbing back towards the arcade. The spiders' numbers grew and grew until Sarah could only see the redness of their eyes overtaking the shadowy tunnel. They climbed as quickly as possible, but the spiders were gaining. The distance slowly closed. Sarah began to hear the snapping of their fangs, and felt the crashing of their knife-like legs chipping the rocky floor.

Suddenly Samuel tripped, slipping in a small puddle of green slime, and came crashing down behind them. Sarah knelt behind him, swinging the flame, warding the spiders away in fear, but their numbers were quickly growing. However many she swung away, two dozen more were taking their place just as quickly. She watched them closing in on the four of them.

Alex ran back to join her, but stopped as the spiders crowded around them, creating a circle of white devils. He pulled Lexi back in between himself and Sarah, who danced the flames around them in a flurry of fire. Alex could easily see them closing the distance, barely able to catch them before they jumped. He felt the sweat flooding down his forehead as the bigger spiders crawled across the ceiling.

There was yet another loud hissing sound. It cracked through the walls, so loud even the spiders seemed to react painfully, creeping away in fear. By the time the hissing screech had stopped, the spiders were already crawling down the tunnel back to their home. Alex opened his eyes — the darkness was all there was. The two flaming torches had finally drawn their last breaths, snuffing to a burnt husk. He helped Samuel to his feet, dusting off the remnants of dust and rock from his back.

"What was that?" Asked Lexi "Why did they all run away?"

"Anyone wanna stay and find out?" Asked Samuel, already running towards the exit. The others followed quickly behind, tossing the snuffed torches to the ground.

Sarah pulled the flashlight from her back pocket and lit the way. They had finally reached the employee only area of the game-and-stop. The three were a few feet behind as Samuel burst through the doorway, rushing towards the entrance. Lexi was next to run through the door. Sarah turned to Alex, seeing him staring down the tunnel. She heard him whisper something, but couldn't make out what it was.

"Come on!" She said, grabbing his wrist.

The two pushed through the door, stopping inches behind the other two, who stared in awe down the corridor. It took a moment for Sarah to see what the others were so struck by, but eight enormous red eyes stared down at them from the ceiling, just above that beautiful exit sign. Sarah slowly raised the beam of light along the wall towards the eyes. The soft hissing slowly reappeared, like the sound of tight, constricted breathing.

The legs were enormous. Even though they were bent and distorted around the body, they were easily ten feet long, thick, and hairy. At the end, stabbed deep into the ceiling, were thick claw-like spikes. Its fat, white chelicerae wiggled in excitement, and its twitching eyes darted between the four of them.

As the light passed onto its face, the legs extended, reaching down to the floor and spinning the body around. The giant white spider stared darts at the four of them, snapping its colossal fangs together hungrily. The green slime washed down the chelicerae like a waterfall, dripping down the fangs into a puddle on the floor.

Suddenly there was a strange sound,

and the back of the spider's head flapped open, slabs of skin flopping to the side like a budding flower. A pale arm came out, pushing the beautiful torso up into sight. The silver hair draped over her red, terrifying eyes.

Samuel stared in awe at the beauty of the woman. She reminded him of a model, save for the horrific red eyes and black claw-like nails.

The woman hissed, and the spider took a step towards them, crashing its leg against the wall, nearly bringing it tumbling down altogether. It took another step, crumbling the ground beneath it.

Sarah pulled out her brother's knife, thinking of what she could possibly do against something like this. Samuel fiddled with his pockets, feeling nothing but a small pack of cigarettes and his mother's car keys. Lexi stood frozen, staring into the eight massive eyes of the spider as it slowly approached her. Alex wiped the sweat from his brow, patting at his pockets, in a frantic search for….

"Go," he whispered to them, pulling a small black rod from his back pocket.

"Go where?" Responded Sarah. "If you have any ideas…."

"Go back through the door, and take the arcade around her." His voice was unusually calm. "I might have something of an idea."

"Which is?"

"Shut up and go—take the others and get out of here." He popped the cap off the rod, revealing the small white string at the end. "I'm not asking again."

Their eyes met for a moment. Sarah saw something in him that showed he wouldn't budge. She nodded, grabbing the other two by the collars and pulling them back through the door.

Alex tightened his fingers around the string, staring deeply into the eyes of the spider, now only a few meters away from him. The woman almost seemed to smile at him as the spider's mandibles opened, showing the horrific image of what he assumed was the mouth. He yanked the string out, lighting the flare.

***

"What the hell are we doing?!" Shouted Samuel, weaving between arcade games.

"Getting out of here, now move!" Sarah responded, still dragging the awestruck Lexi by her wrist.

"What about Alex?!"

Sarah wanted to shout back, tell him that Alex would be safe, that he knew what he was doing, but truthfully she didn't know. She burst through the door at the other end of the corridor and glanced back.

The spider was a silhouette in front of a bright red light. She couldn't see him, but she knew he was standing there, just on the opposite side of the spider. It looked as if it was backing away, in some strange fear.

There was a second of silence before the spider screeched as loud as possible. It reared up on its hind legs, showing its face blazing. The hairs on its body singed and lit ablaze. The woman scratched futilely at the flames and the spider's legs danced frantically, crashing through the floor and walls, bursting anything and everything in its way.

Sarah felt the quaking floor. She jumped just in time to avoid the shard of metal crashing down from the ceiling. The rain of rock and metal started, and the walls came tumbling down. She yanked on Lexi's wrist and shoved her and Samuel through the door, following close behind.

***

Alex fell back, the flare bouncing off the spider's face, igniting the thick venom drenching down its fangs. He looked up to see the spider's frenzied dance of pain, as the flames travelled down its legs and up its bulbous abdomen.

A shard of stone crashed to the ground a foot away from him, sending shrapnel into his arm. He clenched the spot, glancing up to see the falling roof raining towards him, and began running towards the spider. The hectic stomping legs crashed all around him. He tried his best to weave through the small openings he had. He felt a flame slap against his face, searing a small burn on his cheek, but eventually he made his way towards the door, bursting through just before the building crumbled to the ground atop the beastly mama spider.

"Alex?" Sarah asked, the dust finally settling in front of the old Mark's Game-and-Stop.

"I hate spiders," Alex said, coughing out the last remnants of the old building.

He appeared limping from the cloud of debris, gripping tightly on his stained red arm. Sarah was the first to rush towards him, but soon enough the rest of them were all included in the embrace.

**

Midnight. The moon stared down at the

crumbled remains of the old game shop. The bright orange sports car sat quietly in the parking space. The silver lighter flicked open, igniting the small dancing flame before snuffing it out once again. The burned face stared down at the small crumbled pieces of rock and stone that had once stood as a reminder of the old arcade. Alex leaned against the hood of his car, watching out the corner of his eye as the black limousine drove off into the distance.

He stood for a moment staring up at the moon, thinking of the past few nights. The friends he'd lost, the terrors he'd seen. He shut the lighter and stuffed it into his pocket. A few seconds later he noticed the black van driving over the curb ungracefully and parking in the spot next to him.

"Funny seeing you girls here," he said as Lexi rolled down the window.

"You too," Sarah said from the passenger's seat.

"I gotta say, Leo," Lexi said, eyeing

Alex's face closely, "that new burn mark really works for ya. Gives you a dangerous look." She winked.

"Think it'll help with the ladies?" He asked, looking at himself in his reflection.

"Like *you* need any help there," responded Sarah with a grin. "Come to say goodbye?"

"Yeah, my brother's waiting at home for me — we'll be leaving in the morning. What about you guys?"

"I'm moving out of this town," Lexi responded, fiddling with her hands at the wheel. "After all this, I don't think I can stay here."

"I don't really have a place to stay right now," Sarah said, fiddling with the silver half-heart pendant between her fingers. "So I'm going to room with Kit for a while until I figure things out."

"Any idea where you'll go next?" Asked Alex.

"Not sure, probably somewhere down

south. What about K9?"

"He's stuck here for a while—gotta take care of his sisters, you know. But I'm sure he'll be out of here soon enough."

"Maybe we'll meet somewhere soon," said Sarah, threading the silver chain through the pendant. "Here." She tossed it out the window at him.

"It's not mine, though," he responded, confused.

"It is now. None of us would be here if you hadn't figured out how to fight that.... Well anyway, I want you to have it, and I'd better see it on you next time we meet up for lunch."

"You bet." He pulled the chain over his head, letting the pendant rest on his chest. "Take care, you two. And let's make a deal not to run through abandoned buildings anymore."

"Deal," the two girls said, a small laugh seeping through.

Lexi flicked the keys and started out

towards the horizon, leaving Alex in the lot alone. He fingered the small pendant, running his thumb along the jagged edge before opening his own car door. The keys hung from the ignition loosely. He watched as a tiny brown spider descended from his rear-view mirror. He stuck a hand out, allowing the spider to sit calmly in his palm, before opening the window and letting it crawl onto the ground outside the door.

There was a ringing coming from his glove compartment. He pulled out the small black flip phone and answered.

"Agent Six," he answered. "Oh, hello, ma'am. I hadn't expected your call, the debrief team just left a moment ago. Well of course, the cryptid was dealt with tonight, as I promised this morning. I handled it myself. Make sure Emily knows I can handle myself from time to time—I've been doing this longer than she has, after all. The office? Yes, there were several research notes on a cryptid named 'Crypto-Aranea.' Or as I

159

would put it, 'Giant Freaking Spider.' Yes, that information would have been more useful before I began this whole operation, but it's over now. Oh, there was one other thing in the office." He reached into the glove compartment and pulled out the brown envelope, the wax seal now broken. "An envelope addressed to the good doctor. Yes, I believe he was here recently, come to check on his pet. The back was sealed with a black D. Does that mean anything to you? Yes, of course, ma'am. Regardless, inside were more research notes on another of LeCrane's cryptids called 'Crypto-Feralis Bruti' in a town not far from here. Somewhere called Cold Stone. Probably a day's ride east." He shoved the papers back in the glove compartment and shut the door. "Yeah, tell the girls I'll meet them there. Anyway, long drive ahead, Six out." He clapped the phone shut and tossed it on the passenger's seat.

Alex cranked the keys to the side, roaring the car to life, and pumped it several times, feeling the hard growl of the engine shake his bones back and forth. He flicked through the radio, finally deciding on a nice hard rock channel.

"Fitting," he chuckled, brushing a lock of hair from in front of his eyes.

He pulled back on the shift and burst out of the parking lot, drifting onto the Ghost Street. The wind rushed through the windows and blew his hair back as the pale moonlight stared down.

FIN...?